MRS CARTERET RECEIVES

AND OTHER STORIES

L. P. HARTLEY

MRS CARTERET RECEIVES

AND OTHER STORIES

HAMISH HAMILTON
LONDON

First published in Great Britain 1971
by Hamish Hamilton Ltd
90 Great Russell Street London WC1
Copyright © 1971 by L. P. Hartley

SBN 241 02040 9

For Margaret and Ralph
with much affection
from
Leslie

Printed in Great Britain by
Western Printing Services Ltd, Bristol

CONTENTS

CONTENTS

ACKNOWLEDGMENTS

Most of the stories in this collection are here published for the first time but some have previously appeared in *Vogue*, The *Contemporary Review* and the *Sixth Ghost Book* (Barrie & Jenkins, London), to whom my thanks are due for permission to reprint them.

L.P.H.

MRS CARTERET RECEIVES

FROM the social angle, as Proust might have seen it, the great cities of Italy have no counterpart in England. In England there were hierarchies still at the turn of the century and later, as long as each town, large or small, was an entity in itself only to be approached from outside by a long, laborious and possibly hazardous journey in a horse-and-trap or wagonette.

In such towns there were ranks, conditions and degrees; and a newcomer, be he doctor, solicitor, farmer, or someone not actively engaged in 'trade', was carefully vetted before he was admitted into the social club, the tennis club, the cricket club, the Masons', the Foresters', or any of the many clubs where men congregate to keep each other in, and outsiders out.

All this sounds very snobbish, but it was really not so; for certainly in the smaller towns everyone knew everyone else and was hail-fellow-well-met with him; there were no Trades Unions; the carpenter was satisfied with being a carpenter, and had no feeling of inferiority or envy when he talked to a white-clad member of the tennis club (perhaps lately elected) swinging his racquet. There was a kind of democracy based on neighbour-liness and familiarity. Enter the motor-car, with its money-borne social distinctions and its capacity to move its owner and his family from a dull town to a gayer one, and this democracy of place and local habitations began to wane.

Not so in the great cities and even the smaller towns of Italy. There the bourgeoisie had, and no doubt still have, their social rivalries, their jockeying for place, their intrigues, their equivalents for keeping up with the Jones's (though it must be said that most Latin countries, if not so democratically governed, are

socially more democratically-minded, than we are, and this is true
of all ranks of society). They have not a common parlance, a
lingua franca, indeed they have not, least of all in Venice where
only a few of the aristocracy can speak the dialect of the *popolo*,
which is almost a separate language. At the same time a duchess
could talk more freely to a window-cleaner (if such exists in
Venice), and with less sense of the barriers of class than she could
here. The Venetian *popolo* has very little sense of social or intel-
lectual inferiority; a cat can look at a king, and address him too.
But they have a very strong sense of pecuniary inequality.
'*Questa Duchessa ha molti millioni*' (This Duchess has many
millions) and of this discrepancy they take what advantage they
can, as their employers, should they be private or public, well
know.

But what I wanted to say was that the social system of Italy in
its upper reaches such as would have appealed to Proust, differed
from ours in being predominantly urban, not rural. The great
families, the Colonna, the Orsini, the Caetanis, the Medicis, the
Sforzas, the Estes, the Gonzagas, the Contarinis and Mocenigos,
had and no doubt still have, great estates in the country, but the
centre of their lives, their *point d'appui*, was urban, in the city to
which they belonged and over which they ruled.

In England, noble families are seldom denizens of the towns or
counties from which they take their titles. The Duke of Norfolk
doesn't live in Norfolk; the Duke of Devonshire doesn't live in
Devonshire; the Duke of Bedford doesn't live in Bedford; the
Duke of Northumberland does live in Northumberland, but
Northumberland is a large county, and many people would not
know that his home town was Alnwick, where his castle is.

At the time of which I write, bridging perhaps half a century
between 1890 and 1940, English people, emigrants or semi-
emigrants, had established a hold, based on affinity, in many cities
of Italy, chiefly Rome, Florence and Venice. Others went further
afield; but the lure of Italy, for many English people, especially
those with aesthetic tastes, was irresistible.

'Open my heart, and you will see graved inside of it, Italy,' wrote Robert Browning; and how many of his compatriots have re-echoed those sentiments. The Italians, great and small, seemed to re-echo them too. There was a genuine feeling of affection, based on more than mutual advantage, between the two nations. I remember my gondolier saying to me when the troublous relationships between our two countries began over Sanctions, 'There was a time when an Englishman was a king in Venice.'

But that was much later.

Going back to earlier years and adopting (as far as one can!) a Proustian outlook of the upper ranks of 'Society', and how they comported themselves, one heard of the Anglo-American colony in Venice, residents with beautiful houses. They were completely different from and slightly aghast at the rash of moneyed visitors who invaded Venice after the First World War, a cosmopolitan crowd who thronged the Lido, behaved anyhow in the Piazza, and at a given date—dictated by fashion—departed one and all to an hotel on Lake Como. These rather noisy immigrants were called by the Italians 'The Settembrini', and various odd and irregular modes of behaviour were attributed to them.

As it happened this post-war violation of Venice coincided with, though it did not cause, the exit from the city of the older and stabler foreign colony. Some died; some just went away, and these included several distinguished ladies, titled and untitled, who had made Venice their second home, and had there entertained many eminent literary figures, some from foreign countries including Henry James, and also including (last and least) Baron Corvo, who bit the hand that fed and lent him money.

It cannot be supposed that the Italians, to whom Venice belonged, were socially inactive during this time; but they had no tradition of hospitality except possibly between themselves; they accepted hospitality from guest-hungry *forestieri*, but they didn't always return it. They had indeed a queen, a social sovereign, who, besides being a famous beauty, and the favourite, it was said, of a King, enjoyed playing bridge more than entertaining the bridge-players to dinner.

The Anglo-American colony, though now sadly diminished in

strength and numbers and money, closed their ranks and were still the only section of the Venetian community who said to their friends—Venetians or foreign—'Will you come and have tea with me?'

Now Mr. and Mrs. Carteret, in their narrow and narrowing orbit, reigned supreme.

They had come to Venice in the last decade of the nineteenth century. Why they had taken this step of expatriation I do not know.

He was an American from New England, whose original name was Carter; she was a Jewess called Hannah Filkenstein from New York, whose family (they were bankers) was, it was said—and this was confirmed by many people who didn't like her—the first Jewish family to be received in the best New York society. She was one of the 400; 'I should not be here,' she said once, 'if it wasn't from having some holes and corners in New York.'

How James Carteret and Hannah Filkenstein ever met was never explained, still less why they married. It was said, of course, that he married her for her money; but he had money of his own. He was a small, rather chétif-looking man with a moustache (his wife once said to me 'No man can afford to be without a moustache'); he had a nervous manner and a high-pitched laugh. 'Oh don't, don't, don't, don't, don't,' he used to say, after any remark made by him or anyone else which had the faintest element of humour in it—as though the effort to laugh was more than he could bear.

He was a *petit maître*, literally and figuratively. He had exquisite taste and a talent as a painter in the style of Sargent. This he abandoned when he married. If his friends reproached him he would say, 'I gave up painting when I began to mingle with the rich and great.'

His wife had not his talents, but she was a very cultivated woman who spoke French and Italian (and probably German) rather slowly, as she always spoke, but quite correctly, and who read a great deal, though she would not always admit to this.

Together they occupied the Palazzo Contarini dal Molo; not a typical Venetian palazzo, but with the most beautiful view in Venice, and perhaps in the world; for being on the north side it overlooked the inward curve of the Fondamenta Nuove, on the Laguna Morta; and further to the left on the cemetery of San Michele (too beautiful to be thought of as a cemetery) and then towards Murano and Burrano. Those who had eyes to see could see what Guardi, one of whose favourite subjects it was, had seen.

But the view was not the only beauty of the Palazzo Contarini dal Molo. It had its garden. There are few gardens in Venice and this had a rival on the Giudecca; but it is, or was, the most beautiful. It was designed by Palladio or Sansovino, I forget which, and ran down a couple of hundred yards, with the lagoon lapping it, until it was outflanked by a dusty-red building on the right-hand corner. 'The Casino degli Spiriti' it was called. It was said to be haunted, hence the name; it was also said to have been Titian's studio, but no one was ever asked to go inside it. Some said it was empty and there was nothing to see.

But the greatest of the many beauties which emanated from the palace and to which, so to speak, it held the key, the enchantments over which it waved its wand, was the palace itself. Not outside; it was not a typical Venetian palace, towering upwards within a riot of ornament and embellishment; outside it was low and plain and unadorned, and might have been mistaken for a warehouse or even a workhouse. Oh, how different now from its former aspect! 'C'erano tante famiglie, tante, tante,' my gondolier used to say, occupying the palace before Mr. Carteret came and turned them out. Seeing its possibilities he took it over and transformed it into the vision of beauty it afterwards became.

My gondolier was obviously in sympathy with the 'tantissime famiglie' who had been evicted by the Carterets; but nothing succeeds like success, and many Italians, high and low, cannot resist its allure. The Carterets had made their will prevail, and others less fortunate than they (such is Fate, and the Italians have a great regard for Fate) must fend for themselves.

And so it came about that the Palazzo Contarini dal Molo, which had been occupied by tantissime famiglie, in indescribable squalor, was now occupied by two persons with a suitable number of retainers, in great grandeur. The moment one was admitted by the butler (who was also the Carterets' first gondolier, but so transformed by his black clothes that no one who didn't know would have recognized him) everything changed. He might have been admitting the guest into a church, so solemn and reverential was his demeanour as he walked rather slowly up the unimpressive staircase, keeping to the right, and treading softly as though on holy ground.

But when the door of the ante-room was opened, what a change! What a vision of beauty, subdued, protected from the vulgar encroachments of the sunshine by ruched honey-coloured blinds, drawn half-way down. And from the midst of this luminous twilight would appear Mrs. Carteret wearing, as often as not, the broad-brimmed straw hat which cast a shadow over the upper part of her face.

'Oh, it is you!' she would exclaim, with a faint air of surprise. 'I hardly expected you, but here you are!' (The element of surprise was never quite absent from her manner.) 'I was afraid some other engagement might have kept you, as it did once before, do you remember?' The embarrassed guest tried to remember an occasion when he had let down Mrs. Carteret, but couldn't, and at that moment Mr. Carteret, who had been somewhere in the shadows eclipsed by the ample form and wide-spreading hat of Mrs. Carteret, came to his rescue.

'We are so glad to see you,' he said, with the beginnings of a titter that seldom left his lips. 'Venice is quite a desert now since the dear Hohenlohes, and Lady Malcolm and Mrs. Frontisham died or went away—so we have found no one to meet you, alas!' And in the minutes following five more guests were ushered in, all with the most resounding names.

They looked about them—it was impossible not to, so great was the prestige with which the Carterets had contrived to invest their house—and then they followed Mrs. Carteret and her pale-blue silk fichu (meant for the cold or the heat?) into the dining-room, but not before aperitifs had been offered. These, though exiguous, were quite delicious, and I once asked Mr. Carteret what was the recipe. He hesitated long enough for me to feel I had made a *gaffe*, and then said, 'Please don't mind, but I think people might . . . might talk if two Englishmen in Venice served the same cocktail. Oh don't, don't, don't, don't, don't!'

With that and the cocktail I had to be content, although Mr. Carteret was only a recent Englishman, having changed his nationality for reasons best known to him, and his wife had followed suit.

All the rooms in the house were low by Venetian standards, but the Carterets' dining-room had a ceiling by Tiepolo which one could not help looking at, so near was it to one's head. It depicted the glorification of someone—perhaps a prevision of Mrs. Carteret?—with angels, saints and *putti* assisting at the apotheosis.

Mrs. Carteret did not like the ceiling to be remarked on, but equally she did not like it not to be remarked on. With her, it was always difficult to get things right.

Course followed course; the cooking was excellent, the service beyond praise. At the end Mrs. Carteret might say, 'I'm afraid we have had a rather frugal meal—the cook is ill, as she sometimes is—so tiresome—so we have to rely on the kitchen-maid.'

No, it may have been a perhaps perverted and unrealizable wish on the part of Anna (née Hannah) to keep up standards, of whatever sort, that made her look so critically on the outside world. From her ivory tower she could afford, in every sense of the word, to do so. So-and-so was common (a word she was not afraid to use), so-and-so was stupid, so-and-so was ugly, so-and-so could not speak French and above all, so-and-so had no introduction to her.

Anathema! Away with them, and leave the world clearer for Carteret standards to prevail. In the provincial city of Venice (though she did not regard it as such) it was easier to make her considerable weight felt than in the capitals of Europe. So when a well-known couple, whose relationship was irregular, but who had a letter of introduction to her, asked what day would be convenient to call, she replied 'No day would be convenient.'

Snubs to you, and snubs all round, except to a few individuals who satisfied Mrs. Carteret's exacting conception of what is *comme il faut*, and even they were liable to fall from grace. I remember an instance. A friend who had every qualification for enjoying Mrs. Carteret's esteem appeared at dinner in a slightly décolleté dress (it wouldn't have seemed so now) and Mrs. Carteret, a storm on the rugged terrain of her features, rose and asked the guest to put on a shawl. She was not received again, even if she had wanted to be.

Receive, receive!

She herself had been received first into the Jewish Church, then into the Anglican Church, then into the Roman Catholic Church. What a number of receptions, each inflating her ego. No more receptions were in sight, except from the Pope.

Meanwhile her rôle was to make reception, as far as she was concerned, a stumbling-block.

'*Procul O procul este, profani!*'

The profane vulgar must be kept away, they would never climb the heights, or go through the initiations, that she had.

*

She rose to her feet, a rather formidable escalation, very unlike Venus rising from the waves, and supported by her husband's fragile arm, said, 'We will have coffee in the drawing-room.'

The drawing-room was well worth waiting for; it was the most beautiful room in the house and some might have said the most beautiful room in Venice. It stretched the whole breadth of the building and looked out, on one side, on the long crescent curve of the Fondamenta Nuove, with the slender campanile of San Francesco della Vigna dividing it; and on the other side, the Laguna Morta, with the sad but exquisite cemetery of San Michele, and Murano and Burrano somewhere behind it.

'You mustn't let your coffee get cold,' Mrs. Carteret would say as her guests pressed their noses against the windows.

Thereupon they turned back into the room itself, which was painted or stuccoed in an indescribable shade of blue, at once dark and light, the changeful blue of the Italian skies, a perfect background for the tapestries and Chinese screens on the walls.

Sometimes Mrs. Carteret would say, when coffee and liqueurs were over, 'Would you like to take a stroll in the garden?' much as God might have said it of Eden, and the guests, already bemused by the heady qualities of the house, would follow her down the few steps that led to the garden, Mrs. Carteret preceding them, with careful footsteps. Dressed in beige, or some light colour with a tinge of pink in it (for in spite of her bulk she preferred light colours) she would lead the way, and someone said of her, a quotation I have never been able to trace, 'She hath a monstrous beauty, like the hind-quarters of an elephant.'

When we reached the fountain (Sansovino? Palladio?) which was the centre of the garden, she might say,

'I don't expect you want to go any further. Further on you can see the usual mixture of sandole and bragozze, fishermen plying their trade. I don't think they're very interesting.' And sometimes she would add, 'We have a gardener, but there aren't many flowers in the garden. Italians are not flower-minded. If you point to a rose and ask them what it is, they will say '*È un fiore*'—'it's a flower'—but they don't get any further than that.'

By then it was clearly time to go, although luncheon in Italy, with its aftermath, drags on for at least two hours before it is polite to leave.

*

How the Carterets acquired the Palazzo Contarini dal Molo I never knew. It must have been at some time when houses in Venice were cheaper than they are now. Also, it was far off the beaten track; from where I stayed, on the other side of Venice, the sunny side, it needed half an hour on foot or in gondola to get there.

James Carteret, I am sure, espied its possibilities; his was the artist's eye; and its connection with the Contarini family, to whom it had once belonged, no doubt endeared it to him. The Contarinis, after having seven Doges to their name, against the Mocenigos' six, were now extinct. Their last surviving member, at a party, claimed the privilege of going in last. 'All Venice,' he said, 'is my house.'

The Carterets were nothing if not snobs—he a genealogical snob, and she a social one. His name had originally been Carter, of an esteemed New England family. He did not think it imposing enough and when he came to Venice he added the 'et' that turned it to Carteret, the name of a distinguished English statesman. As time passed he persuaded himself and tried to persuade others that he was collaterally descended from the Carterets, and had only omitted the 'et' in deference to New England democratic feeling. The Anglo-American colony, or what remained of it, and some of the Italians, who were in touch with it, made jokes about this—'Carter-et-, et quoi?' or 'Carter-et cetera, et cetera.' His wife, who had been Hannah Filkenstein, followed suit by changing her first name to Anna. This too aroused ribald jokes in the select circles of Venice.

'My dear, have you taken to dropping your h's? You mean Hannah, not Anna.'

But none of these pinpricks pierced the Carterets, who were far too secure with their money and the beauty that they had bought and made for themselves, and that lay within and around them, and with the visitors to Venice who came with introductions and were received by Anna Carteret with varying degrees of welcome. I should never have been received in those hallowed precincts, but for my travelling companion, who had an introduction to her and who bore a well-known name, as a result of which a visiting-card inscribed in the most beautiful copper-plate, 'Mr. James Carteret', invited us both in an almost illegible handwriting, to lunch. We seemed to pass the test, at least he did, and when after some years he ceased to be a frequent visitor to Venice, Mrs. Carteret did not withdraw her favour (not her favours) from me, except on certain occasions.

I had formed the habit of lunching in my gondola in the lagoon —a picnic lunch—but it was delightful, and being young then, or comparatively young, I hated to forgo it. Mrs. Carteret, being old or comparatively old, much preferred having guests to lunch than to dinner. 'A mon âge,' she used to say, for the French language had then the chic which ours has not, 'I would rather lunch than dine,' and it is still a grief to me that I would not always fall in with her wishes. What did it matter, sacrificing a lunch on the lagoon by some dreary uninhabited island, when I could have had it with her and her guests ('no one to speak of') to the music of the plashing of the Palladio fountain? For she, like me, was fond of lunching out-of-doors, and the food appeared as though by magic still hot from the inside of the house.

But I did not always refuse these invitations to lunch, which were after all most acceptable and accompanied by amenities of company, food and service that I could never have provided for myself. But still I was unwilling to forgo my daily stint on the lagoon, on which I imagined my physical and mental health depended. During these exertions I worked up a tremendous sweat, and having been warned by my mother that it was dangerous to sit (possibly in a draught) in sweat-soaked clothes—when I was bidden to lunch with Mrs. Carteret I used to take a supply of dry garments, and ask if I might change in the gondoliers' room.

'But what do you *do* there?' she would ask, having given me permission. 'Wouldn't you rather go upstairs and be more comfortable in a bathroom?'

It was a pertinent question, for nothing could be less like the inside of the palazzo, designed for show, than the gondoliers' room, designed (if designed at all) for use. My plan was really easier and in the end she gave way to it.

In one corner there was a small wash-basin which did not admit hot water, where the two gondoliers presumably refreshed their bodies after their labours at the oar, before they presented themselves as model men-servants in the chambers above. A slight smell of what? of unwashed bodies—lingered around, for the gondoliers, and who could blame them?—did not always have the time or the inclination to transform themselves, skin-high, from their aquatic to their domestic rôles. Some guests (of whom I was not one) remarked maliciously of an effluvium of perspiration; but then Venice is so full of smells.

The gondoliers' room was not meant to be seen by the guests at the Palazzo Contarini dal Molo. Indeed it is doubtful if Mr. and Mrs. Carteret had ever seen it. It was, as far as it was anything, severely utilitarian. There were some ash-trays here and there, perhaps with the name of the hotel they came from on them, and some coat-hangers ditto, on which the gondoliers hung their walking-out clothes. There were a couple of stiff-backed chairs, not affording much relaxation to a tired man, a table or two and the remains of a carpet, which may have been in the palazzo before the Carterets bought it.

It wasn't a small room, for few rooms in Venice are small; and it had an unshaded light-bulb hanging from the ceiling, leaving the corners in a mysterious gloom, relieved, or unrelieved, by dim forms that one didn't want to see, and that I seldom saw because I usually came by daylight.

The gondoliers didn't seem to realize the squalor of their surroundings, they were invariably pleasant and invariably brought me a clean towel, and I, 'à mon âge', as Mrs. Carteret would have said, didn't mind the cold water, it was rather refreshing after the ardours and endurances of the lagoon.

Sometimes my gondolier would come and chat to the other two (for all the gondoliers know each other, even if they don't always like each other) in their dialect which I couldn't understand, though the word 'soldi, soldi' ('money, money') kept recurring. Beyond giving me a clean towel and the vest and shirt my gondolier had brought with him, they paid no attention to me, and chattered to each other, almost regardless of my presence. Then suddenly Antonio would get up, put on his black suit and say, almost reproachfully, 'La signora lei aspetta,' ('Madam is expecting you') and usher me to the upper regions.

Oh, what a change was there!

*

As the years passed Mr. and Mrs. Carteret became ever more conscious of their social position. They relaxed it in the case of certain people with high-sounding names, 'Those poor *realis* of—' she said, referring to certain royal personages visiting Venice who had not a very good name. And when a woman of rank and title came to Venice and stayed with some Lido-loungers of whom Mrs. Carteret did not approve, she said, 'When a woman of her position, or the position she once had, goes to France and becomes *déclassée*, and then comes to Venice and stays with riff-raff —I don't call that very interesting.'

Interesting it was—but Mrs. Carteret could not equate 'interesting' with what was not *comme il faut*. At least in certain moods she couldn't, or wouldn't. But it was hard to tell what she was thinking, for her eyes were enigmatic under the shadow of that broad-brimmed hat; and when the 'riff-raff' who had taken for the season one of the largest palaces on the Grand Canal invited the Carterets to meet their distinguished guest the Carterets accepted, and I remember meeting 'Anna' as I had come to call her (though I don't think she liked the familiarity) at the top of the grand staircase, beneath the loudest clap of thunder I ever heard.

Afterwards she asked the guest who had demeaned herself by staying with the 'riff-raff' to dinner, but she did not ask them.

No fry was too small or too great to be exempt from Mrs. Carteret's liberal disapproval. Whether her attitude came from some long-hidden inferiority complex who can say? There was no need for it; the Filkensteins were the first Jewish family to be received into New York society; and Carter was a well-known and respected name in New England, before he added 'et' to it.

Whatever the reason, Anna Carteret enjoyed putting people in their place. It was said that her husband, with his high-pitched laugh and his slight figure, half the size of hers, had his way in matters that were really important; perhaps it was he who bought the palazzo, as it was he who decorated it. She had the intelligence and the personality and the culture but he had the taste and the talent and perhaps the will-power under that fragile exterior, ornamented by an over-large grey moustache. 'No man can afford to do without a moustache.' Perhaps it was a secret symbol of authority.

But to the onlooker, it was Mrs. Carteret who ruled the roost, and above all she who decided who should be received or not received.

'Received' was a word that loomed large with her. It implied a moral as well as a social standard, though she relaxed it in the case of certain eminent persons, not only 'the poor *realis* of—' but even of celebrities such as D'Annunzio. 'He's like a spider,' she said with a shudder, as far as that massive frame could shudder, and turned up her nose as far as she could, but she received him all the same.

Others were less fortunate. She had an old friend who had a house in Venice, to which he sometimes repaired, and whose social status was impeccable in England and in Venice, indeed it was by genealogical standards much higher than hers. But they had a tiff—about what I don't remember—but I expect it was a trifle, and they were for a time estranged. When he, who was as elderly as she, wanted to bring this misunderstanding to an end he wrote and asked if on a certain day he might come and call on her. To which she replied, that most unfortunately, on the day he suggested she was 'giving' a children's party, and there were no more chairs. It was unlikely that she had ever spoken to a child, much less entertained one.

This, to Sir Ronald, who knew the house well, and who knew that Mrs. Carteret would never give a children's party as she knew no children, and that even if she did there would still be at least a hundred unoccupied chairs in the palazzo, was an offence. But he gave way, as most people did, to Mrs. Carteret for she had the whip-hand. I am glad to say their quarrel was afterwards patched up.

Then I, after several years of happy relationships with Mrs. Carteret, fell foul of her. It was my fault, I should have known. My parents came to stay with me in Venice, and I thought they should be shown one of its less known but more beautiful sights, the Palazzo Contarini dal Molo.

I should have known that my parents could be of no possible interest to Mr. and Mrs. Carteret socially, genealogically, or publicly.

Mrs. Carteret was most gracious, she asked us to lunch, and she and James even came to lunch with us, in our palazzino. My parents stayed for three weeks, and towards the end of their visit I thought it only civil to ask Madame Carteret if we could pay her a farewell visit, not a *visite de digestion*, but just an acknowledgement of her kindness in having received us.

I suggested a day a week or more ahead, but a telephone message came from Mrs. Carteret saying she was very sorry but she could not receive us as the garden was too wet.

Would it have been too wet in a week's time? Or would its humidity have interfered with our call, which had no connection with the garden?

(A propos, Mrs. Carteret sometimes complained that her guests came to see her only because they wanted to see the garden; or, alternatively, that when they came they never cast an eye on the garden (Palladio? Sansovino?), which was one of the treasures of Venice.)

I was offended by her refusal to see my parents again on such a feeble, pseudo-meteorological excuse, but I realized that I had mistaken her nature, and it was my fault, more than hers.

No, it may have been a perhaps perverted and unrealizable wish on the part of Anna (Hannah) to keep up standards, of whatever sort that made her look so critically on the outside world. From her ivory tower she could afford to, in every sense of the word.

Another episode occurs to me. An old friend of mine and an old acquaintance of Mrs. Carteret's, came to stay with me. In her beautiful house in Chelsea she kept a salon to which the old, and even more the young, were only too glad to be invited.

When I asked Mrs. Carteret if I might bring my old friend (and hers) to call, her brow furrowed. 'This Boadicea of the South,' she said, 'cannot possibly receive this Messalina of the North—' and she added in a lower tone, and with a slight closing of the eyelids, 'You know how quickly news travels in Venice. When I told my dear Maria that the daughter of an eminent Bishop might be coming to lunch, she replied, "But Signora, how can a Bishop possibly have a daughter?".'

'She is not staying here,' said Mrs. Carteret, to make the position perfectly plain, 'she is staying with a friend whom you know.' (She didn't mention my name.) 'It is not for us to judge. Of course, heretics have different ideas from ours, but many of them are good people according to their lights, and so on Friday (no, not on Friday, which is a fast day for us) we will have —' and a long list of comestibles permitted by the Church followed.

But it must not be supposed that Mr. and Mrs. Carteret satisfied their romantic longings by receiving the more important visitors to Venice or (by what gave them perhaps greater pleasure) refusing to receive those who were less important. Their romanticism went further than the bounds of snobbery and super-snobbery in which to some extent it fulfilled itself.

Mr. Carteret had his pictures on the walls of the ante-room. He had no reason to be ashamed of them and when visitors praised them and asked him why he had given up painting—'Oh don't, don't, don't, don't!'—he would exclaim, and make his usual excuse for having stopped painting when he began to mingle with the rich and great.

Mrs. Carteret owed no apologies to anyone. She did not feel the need to exhibit her rather laborious knowledge of foreign languages, accurate and impressive as it was, and acquired—who knows how?—in holes and corners of New York, or her considerable knowledge of art and literature which she perhaps felt was beneath her, to any so-and-so who had been admitted to her presence.

In her case, as in his, this was a kind of negative romanticism, the rich, cultured, high-born American keeping the profane, vulgar, at bay.

Yet true romanticism demands more than negation and disapproval: it demands a positive gesture, something creative, something to hand down to the ages.

It happened before my time, and how it happened I never knew, but rumour told me it happened this wise. Mr. and Mrs. Carteret gave an evening party after dinner in the height of summer, to which everyone who was anyone was invited.

Refreshments no doubt were served, perhaps under the light of gondola lanterns, antique and modern: I can imagine their ghostly glimmering.

As the warm evening drew to its close, and the mosquitoes began to make their unwelcome attentions, there was a sudden movement, and there emerged from among the bushes, towards and around the fountain, a rush, a displacement of air quite indescribable—and there, said the guests, who could none of them afterwards agree, were a nymph and a shepherd, representing Mrs. and Mr. Carteret. For two or three minutes, hand in hand and foot by foot, they encircled the dim sub-aqueous shimmer of the fountain, frolicking and kicking their heels. Then other lights were turned on, fairy-lights away in the garden, and Mr. and Mrs. Carteret in a guise that was never agreed upon, ushered their guests out.

So no one ever knew for certain, though speculations were rife, what costumes Mr. and Mrs. Carteret had worn for their middle-aged pastoral idyll. Some went so far as to say they had worn nothing; while others said the whole thing was a hoax and the figures, clothed or unclothed, that issued from the bushes and danced round the fountain had been hired by Mr. and Mrs. Carteret to give the impression of an old-time Venetian *bal masqué*?

Was this extraordinary exhibition the object of the party—to show Mr. and Mrs. Carteret in their primeval youth?

The guests never knew; they made their farewells and their exits not knowing what to say, and leaving the shepherd and the shepherdess in the darkness.

The incident was often referred to by their friends, but not by Mr. and Mrs. Carteret. They lived out, and outlived, their innate earlier romanticism and did not repeat the experiment. There were no more shepherds and shepherdesses in the garden (Palladio? Sansovino?). Only properly attired fashionable guests (with *one* exception) were entertained there.

*

Among the yearly visitors to the Palazzo Contarini dal Molo, was

one who always escaped Mrs. Carteret's lively censure. This was
Princess X, who came from a distant mid-European country, but
who sometimes deigned to set foot in Venice. For Mrs. Carteret,
Princess X could do no wrong. In the early autumn I used to be
warned, 'Someone interesting is coming to stay with us. I hope
you will be here.' The 'someone' was never mentioned by name,
but I knew who she was. Her sojourns at the Palazzo Contarini
dal Molo were brief, but they were much prepared for and looked
forward to. When the princess finally arrived after adequate
arrangements had been made, she did something which Mrs. Carteret would not have tolerated in anyone else. She was at least
half an hour late for every meal. Lateness was something Mrs.
Carteret bitterly resented: as she sometimes said to a belated
guest, 'Better never than late.' But not to Princess X, whose late
appearances were designed to make an impression. Wearing her
famous emeralds, and her fading beauty, she would walk into the
ante-room, looking vaguely around her, as if time was of no
consequence, and Mrs. Carteret would rise laboriously to her
feet and her husband more agilely to his, to greet her.

'Dear Princess!'

This was in the middle and late thirties, before the Abyssinian
War, and Sanctions, which made relationships between our two
countries increasingly difficult. Mr. and Mrs. Carteret, besides
being by birth Americans, were old enough to be above the
battle; they did not much care what happened so long as it did
not happen to them in their secure peninsula of beauty. They
were, if anything, for Mussolini who protected what they stood
and reclined for. But the other Anglo-American inhabitants of
Venice were not in such a happy case, and as the fatal year drew
on, they also withdrew, as I did.

*

Exactly what happened to the Carterets when war was declared
I never knew. Rumours I did hear, many years later, when I came
back to Venice. Mr. Carteret had retired to the South of France,
where he died, leaving the Allied cause a large sum of money.

Anna had predeceased him, perhaps in the first year of the war, perhaps before. We corresponded with each other until letters no longer reached their destination. Our fragile friendship was overwhelmed in the universal cataclysm.

When I went back after the war there were many changes: the Palazzo Contarini dal Molo had passed into other hands, hands as unlike those of its previous owners as could well be imagined. The *suore* (the nuns of Santa Chiara, that noble and austere sisterhood) had bought it, and could there be anything more unlike its present situation and meaning to the world outside than it had in the days of Mr. and Mrs. Carteret? The worldly and the other-worldly could not have been more violently contrasted. The only resemblance between its present and its former owners was the extreme difficulty of being *received*. The nuns, by rules ordained by their illustrious foundress, could not receive people from the outside world. Those who wanted admission had to have special reasons, religious passports so to speak, before they could be let in. In the Carterets' day it had been just as difficult to obtain admittance; but how different were the obstacles then! Then they were purely social; now they were purely spiritual.

But, thought I, the *revenant*, as I walked along the extreme northern fondamenta of Venice, past the Madonna dell' Orto with its wonderful Tintoretto, past the Sacco della Misericordia —hated by the gondoliers in bad weather—and looked down on the long curve of the Fondamenta Nuove—so beautiful, so sunless —and then up at the closed and shuttered windows of the palazzo —is it fair to think that Anna and James Carteret would have minded so much the idea of their cherished and lovely house being occupied by nuns?

Was it quite true that they stood for everything the nuns did not stand for?—for material and snobbish values, and above and beyond them, the values of art and literature, the aesthetic values which they never ceased to uphold and to proclaim?

Looking up at the dull, uninteresting façade of the palace, I thought that never, never again even if the *suore* would receive me, would I venture into those rooms, where beauty had once reigned and which were now dormitories, refectories, toilets, and so on?

Anna Carteret, née Filkenstein, was a Jewess; when she came to Venice she became an Anglican Protestant; after a while she was received into the Roman Catholic Church. Her husband followed at a short distance—*non lungo intervallo*—these religious mutations of hers. It was a grief to the Anglican Church in Venice, to which the Carterets had presented a fine pair of bronze doors, when the Carterets left them and went over to Rome.

These Vicar-of-Bray-like proceedings did, of course, excite hostile comment not only from the faithful Protestants but also from the Italians, who from afar and not much concerned took a cynical view of their tergiversations and said 'I signori Carteret will adopt whatever religion suits them best at the moment.' The Anglican Chaplain felt especially bitter because when the Carterets removed their patronage the Church had to close down.

Well, it was a rather shabby story and yet I could not help feeling that Anna and James had, besides religious snobbery, some better reason for turning their coats so often. Would any one as secure as they were in their social position have changed the forms of their religious faith so often if they hadn't been really interested in religion? They lost face with many people, Protestants and Catholics alike, by doing so. They did not mind such criticism for as Belloc said (*mutatis mutandis*)

> The trouble is that we have got
> The maxim gun, and you have not.

The maxim gun was in their case, of course, money and social prestige. But I couldn't help feeling there was more in their changes of front than that; money and social prestige they could have retained if they had been Jews, Protestants, or anything else. I preferred to think that their changes of mind had been genuine movements of the spirit. But was I right?

Gradually, when I went back to Venice, I began to hear stories —they were not altogether rumours for I knew their gondolier,

Antonio, and I knew their doctor, and I knew Anna's faithful maid and confidante Maria. Their accounts as to what happened to Anna Carteret in her last hours did not always tally, but neither do the Gospels (no levity intended) in their accounts of what happened in the life and death of Jesus Christ, such a different character except in being an outstanding one, and critical of human behaviour—from Mrs. Carteret.

She had seldom been ill, but now, in her late seventies, she was ill, and she knew she was. Her doctor, greatly daring, told her she must stay in bed.

'Is it serious?' asked her husband, who was going to Rome on a mission to the Pope. 'Ought I to stay here?'

'I don't think so,' said the doctor. 'Signora Carteret has a very strong constitution and besides that, she is especially anxious that you should keep this appointment in Rome. I think it would do her more harm if you stayed than if you went. Signora Carteret—'

'I know what you are going to say,' her husband said.

'She doesn't like to be crossed. Speaking as a psychologist, I should say it would be bad for her if you cancelled your visit to Rome. In an illness of this sort,' the doctor didn't give it a name or he was not quite sure what it was, 'as in many other illnesses,' he added hastily, 'it is essential to keep up the patient's interest in life. Mrs. Carteret is, of course, deeply religious and she has set her heart on your being received by His Holiness. Your account of the interview will give her a stronger hold on life than any of my medicines. Equally, disappointment in a matter that means so much to her, would have the opposite effect. She has several times said to me, "I look forward so much to my husband being received by the Pope. It means almost as much to me as if the Holy Father were to receive me myself. My great fear is lest, knowing how concerned James is about my health, he may cancel his appointment and miss this golden opportunity".'

Mr. Carteret thought for a while.

'I shall pray for her as I always have. But would it be correct for me to ask the Holy Father to make intercession for her?'

'Why not?'

'He must have so many reqests of that kind.'

'What if he has?' said the doctor. 'It is part of his business—*il suo mistiere*—to pray for others, and you and your signora have been generous benefactors to the Church.'

'So you think I should go?'

'I do, most decidedly.'

Mr. Carteret went.

*

What happened afterwards is confused and not wholly credible, especially as the evidence of the two eye-witnesses, if such they were, sometimes disagree. If only Dr. Bevilacqua (well-named for he was an ardent teetotaller and could have been relied on to give an accurate account of what happened) had not been called away to another bedside!

Antonio, the Carterets' butler and first gondolier, and Maria, Anna Carteret's personal and confidential maid, were still alive. I sought them out and they remembered me, not I think without affection, as a one-time habitué of the Palazzo Contarini dal Molo.

Their accounts differed in detail but essentially they were the same. Maria and Antonio, the two most favoured servants, may have been jealous or envious of each other. They were not malicious about Mrs. Carteret in spite of her arrogant ways, for she and her husband had left them well provided for.

According to Antonio, the doorbell rang at about 10 p.m., by which time (he said) he would have been in bed but for his concern for the signora. It was a stormy night in November; the north wind, the *bora*, was almost a hurricane. The Carterets' palace received its full force; hardly any gondolier or any sandolier, rowing a working-man's seaworthy boat, would venture down the Sacco della Misericordia, where the wind collected and swept down as in a funnel. The only way to reach the palace on such a dirty night (*una notte così cattiva*) was on foot; and who would want to come then, unless it was the doctor?

Antonio opened the door cautiously and with difficulty, for the wind almost swept it off its hinges and him off his feet; and before he had time to ask who and why, a stranger had slipped in. He was wearing a flimsy raincoat and the red cap that sailors and fishermen sometimes wear; but he was obviously soaked to the skin, and even while he stood a puddle was forming at his feet.

'*Cosa vuole?*' asked Antonio. 'What do you want?'

The man, with water still streaming down his face, said, 'I want to see the signora.'

'I'm afraid you can't,' said Antonio, who was a big burly fellow. '*E impossibile*. La signora is ill—*è molto ammalata*—and she can see nobody.'

'All the same,' said the man who had stopped shivering, 'I think she will see me.'

Antonio glanced at the grotesque looking creature from whose meagre garments the rain was still oozing, and like most Italians, he was not devoid of sympathy for anyone in distress. But what to do for or with this man? A thought occurred to him. '*Rimanga qui*' he said, indicating the gondolier's room where I had so often changed my clothes to make myself presentable to Mrs. Carteret after sweaty expeditions in the lagoon, 'stay here, and I will lend you some dry clothes, and dry yours,' he added, 'and you can spend the night here and no one need know anything about it.' He pushed the man into the gondolier's room. '*Rimanga qui*,' he repeated, 'but I shall have to lock you in.'

But the man said, 'No, I want to see the signora. I have an appointment with her.'

'An appointment?' said Antonio, 'but the signora sees nobody, she is much too ill. And *in ogni caso*—in any case—she receives no one without a written introduction. Do you know her?' he asked, suddenly wondering if this sodden creature might be an old friend of the signora's (for do not many of us come down in the world?) and he, Antonio, might get into trouble for turning him away. 'Do you know her?' he repeated. 'Have you ever met her? What is your name?'

'My name,' said the man. '*Non importa*—it doesn't matter— but she will know me when she sees me.'

Quite what happened then I couldn't make out. Apparently

Antonio pushed the interloper into the gondolier's room, locked the door on him, and went upstairs to consult Maria, whose bedroom had been moved next to Mrs. Carteret's, and who was sitting up more or less all night during her illness.

He explained the situation to Maria.

'*Ma è brutto, sporco, e tutto bagnato,*' he said. 'He is ugly, dirty, and wet through.'

'*Non si può,*' agreed Maria. 'She cannot. But if she gets to hear—and she hears everything—that someone has called to see her and been turned away, ill as she is, she may be very angry.'

The sound of coughing was heard from the next-door room.

'She is awake,' said Maria. 'I will go in and see her—*è il mio dovere*—it is my duty, and say that this person has called.'

She knocked and went into the bedroom, a splendid state-bedroom, where lay under a magnificent four-poster, the ample, but slightly diminished by illness, form of Mrs. Carteret.

'*Cosa vuole?*' she said, with the irritability of a sick person, though she was very fond of Maria. 'What do you want? I was just dropping off to sleep. I was thinking of the signore—not the bon Dieu,' she corrected herself, shaking her head on the pillows, for the 'Signore' was another name for God, 'but Signor Giacomo, who has gone to Rome to be received by the Pope.'

Maria explained, as best she could, why she had butted in.

'What is his name?'

'He would not give it. He told Antonio you would know him when you saw him.'

'Has he a letter of introduction?' asked Mrs. Carteret, whose mind was going back to earlier, happier days.

'No, signora, *è proprio un lazzarone*—a real layabout—and you wouldn't want to see him.'

'Have you seen him, Maria?'

'No, signora, Antonio has locked him up in the gondoliers' room.'

'Tell him, Maria, whoever he is, that I can't possibly receive him. I am much too ill.'

She turned her tired head on the ample pillows and closed her eyes. How unlike the Mrs. Carteret of former days, a travesty of her, a cartoonist's caricature.

*

Maria brought her message, it seems, back to Antonio.

'She cannot receive him,' she said.

'Well, of course not,' said Antonio robustly. 'But we had to ask her—she's so touchy about these things, and he might have been an old boy-friend, *chissà?*—Who knows? And he might be a thief. Anyhow, he was in a bad way, and I gave him some dry clothes and locked him up. I'll let him out in the morning.'

Hardly had he said this when the door—actually there was no door, only curtains of consummate beauty that separated Mrs. Carteret's apartment from the meaner sides of the house (Mr. Carteret had his quarters elsewhere) opened and the stranger, still ugly, still dirty, still dripping, stood before them, an apparition as startling to their thoughts as if they had not been thinking of him, and they turned to each other, dismayed.

'I want to see the signora,' he said.

Antonio was the first to recover himself.

'You can't,' he said. 'La signora is much too ill to see anyone. Go back to where you came from.'

And he took the stranger by the shoulders to push him out. That was his version of the story. Maria was too frightened to remember; but she thought that Antonio's hand closed on something that recoiled, without giving way, and vanished behind the closed door of Mrs. Carteret's bedroom.

*

What next? Presence of mind is a rare quality and Antonio and Maria had spent whatever they had. They leaned their ears against the door and this is what they heard.

'*Chizzè?*'—the Venetian patois for 'Who is it?' The listeners were astonished, they had no idea that Mrs. Carteret knew the Venetian dialect, for though she knew many languages, they did not think that she knew theirs.

It was a deep voice, unlike hers; was she asking him, or he asking her?

The next sentence settled this. 'Who are you? Have you a letter of introduction? I am ill, and I cannot receive anyone without that. My husband is away—he is being received by the Holy Father—and I cannot imagine why my *domestici* let you in. Please go away at once, before I have you turned out.' Her voice, which had been unexpectedly strong, suddenly weakened, 'Who are you, anyway?'

The two outside the door waited for an answer.

A voice in no accent that they knew replied, 'I need no introduction, Signora. I am a common man, *un uomo del popolo*, a man of the people, but sooner or later I get to know everyone. In the end everyone has to receive me, and so must you.'

'Must? I don't understand that word—*non conosco quella parola*—I receive whom I want to receive, and I don't want to receive you.' Her voice grew fainter, but they heard her say 'What is your name?'

They could not hear his answer because he whispered it, perhaps he bent down and whispered it, and a cry pierced the silence, too thin to be called a scream.

Hearing this, Antonio put his shoulder to the door which was unaccountably locked, and went in. The electric light had recovered from the storm and was painfully brilliant; there was no sign of the stranger, but Mrs. Carteret's head had fallen back on the pillow. Was she asleep, or was she—?

They crossed themselves, and Maria closed her eyes. Leaving the bedside Maria noticed the dirty, wet footprints on the floor. 'I'll clean those up,' she said. 'La signora wouldn't have liked them. *Vadi giù*,' she added, 'go down into the gondolier's room and see if the man is still there.'

Key in hand and still looking frightened, Antonio went down to the room which had so often witnessed my post-lagoon ablutions. Coming back he said, '*No, non c'è nessuno.*' 'There is no-one.'

THE SILVER CLOCK

NERINA WILLOUGHBY (so named because her parents, now dead, had liked the flower) had inherited their large house, as was right and proper, for she was their only child. Perhaps on that account she had never married; and was used to being, if not the idol of two people, at least their main object, the centre of their thoughts, and although she had had more than one offer of marriage, she had refused them. She was now thirty-one. Better be an old man's darling than a young man's slave, so ran the proverb; Nerina was good-looking, in a rather austere way, and well-off; her suitors were much younger than she, as perhaps Penelope's suitors were. So far, no middle-aged or elderly *prétendant* had presented himself, and lacking this rather doubtful incentive to matrimony—for though she was sure she didn't want to be a young man's slave—she wasn't quite sure she wanted to be an old man's darling. Her parents had doted on her, their ewe-lamb, much as a middle-aged husband might. But their devotion, in season and out of season, fretted her and demanded of her an obligation of gratitude to which she couldn't always respond and which gave her a feeling of guilt.

Independence, independence! Independence from human ties which are often, as they say, a bind. Better be by oneself, if sometimes lonely, than attached to another human being, probably more selfish than oneself, whose every move of oncoming or withdrawal, and the emotional strain and re-adjustment they entailed, must be met by a corresponding reaction on her part.

And so Nerina, who was far from wanting in affection, in fact too sensitive to its demands and too little inclined to impose her own, took to dog-breeding.

With dogs you knew to some extent where you were. They had their tricks and their manners, as the doll's dressmaker said; no dog was like another, each had to be studied; each had to be cherished; they gave what they had or withheld what they had; but they were, for Nerina, at any rate, objects of devotion on whom she could spend her care and affection without feeling that, sometime or other, they would try to get the upper hand of her. Difficult they often were; but they depended on her, as much as she on them; she never had to say (for at heart she was a disciplinarian) 'I must give way to Rex' (or whatever his name was) as so often women had to, with their husbands.

So Nerina was absorbed in the dogs; they were her interest, her occupation, almost her religion. In this she did not differ from many people who find in animals something they miss in human beings. A sort of *rapprochement*, not always to be relied on, for animals have their moods, as well as we, and sometimes more so, and the discipline, or self-discipline, which we try to impose on them, doesn't always work. An old friend, an animal-lover, once said to her, 'Cats don't see why they should do what you want them to do.' She was not averse to cats, and she recognized and accepted their independence of attitude.

But a dog, it is unnecessary to say, is not like a cat, it is essentially a dependent creature, and needs a great deal of attention paid to it, for which, as a rule, it repays a great deal of attention in return. The relationship is reciprocal but the onus of responsibility lies on the dog's owner. A dog cannot take itself for a walk, or if it does, it is liable to get lost or run over. At stated hours, therefore, it has to be taken out for exercise or to relieve nature which, for some reason, dogs seem to find a more pressing, as well as a more satisfying outlet for their feelings than do other animals.

Nerina's dogs, large shaggy creatures, though not the subject, I hope, for a 'shaggy dog' story, were almost a whole-time job; for besides the daily demands of each adult, for food, exercise, and so on, there were births, marriages and deaths. There were also illnesses; for dogs, perhaps owing to their long association with human beings, were subject to all kinds of epidemics; classic distemper was the most frequent and the worst, but there were always new ones cropping up—hard-pad, for instance—and happily dying down, almost as suddenly as they appeared. Nerina had to be always on the watch, by day and night, for some outbreak of ill-health in the kennels; and so did the vet, for although by this time she had almost as much experience of dog-ailments as he had, she relied on his trained opinion, and, to some extent, on the remedies he prescribed.

This was a bad day in the kennels, for some of the dogs, fifteen of them in all, old, middle-aged, young, and newly-born, had developed symptoms for which she couldn't account and they were clearly spreading. She had, as so often before, summoned the vet, for even if she knew as much about their ailments as he did, it was always better to be on the safe side. However, he couldn't come; he had been called out by the R.S.P.C.A. to separate some fighting swans, or rather to attend to the needs of one who seemed to be dying from the encounter. He didn't want to let down Nerina, who was a good client of his, still less to offend her, for there were other vets besides him, but, as he told her on the telephone, 'you wouldn't believe how often I am called out to deal with fighting swans, especially at this season, when they are mating. I daresay that if they weren't monogamous, they wouldn't get so excited, but they know that if they have set their hearts on a certain female to be their partner for life—their very long life—they say to themselves, "It's either him or me." You would hardly believe how savage they can be—no holds barred. It's twenty miles away, and I shall probably arrive too late, but I may be in time to give the loser an injection, if he'll let me, and the winner a good kick. I don't know why people are so fond of swans—they wouldn't be if they had to assist at their matrimonial proceedings. I'll come on to you directly afterwards, but it may be an hour or two. Meanwhile, from what you say, some salicylate of bismuth might allay the symptoms.'

Nerina had already administered this medicament, and was walking up and down the kennels, which were at a short distance from the garden, which itself was a long distance from the road, to see how effective it had been in staunching the alarming flow from the poor animals' insides, when she looked up and saw five or six youths, between seventeen and nineteen, who were following her movements with eyes that were cold and hard under their long hair.

They were trespassing, of course; but Nerina was too much absorbed in the plight of the dogs to pay much heed to them. She thought of offering them, sarcastically, a dose of salicylate of bismuth, but they appeared not to need it (though her kennel-ground *had* been used, in the past, by interlopers who had been 'taken short'); and she tried to dismiss them from her mind.

But they didn't go away; on the contrary, they came nearer, and as though by a pre-conceived plan, kept pace with her, almost step by step, and only a few yards away, on her sentry-go as she looked into the various kennels to see if the dogs were responding to treatment.

However, after a time this double perambulation, which had the air of an ill-natured mimicry, began to get on her nerves, and deflect her attention from the welfare of the dogs, which was her chief concern.

It was half-past seven in the morning. When she had the dogs to see to, she was oblivious of time; it might have been half-past five. The kennel-maid was away ill; the household, such as it was, was not yet astir; the gardener wasn't due until nine o'clock. Nerina was completely alone.

Meanwhile, the five youths drew still closer, and their attitude, as displayed in their faces and the looks which every now and then they interchanged—sideways and backwards—if not exactly threatening, were anything but friendly.

As a dog-breeder, and a dog-shower, Nerina had seen a good deal of the world and was acquainted with its seamier side, and when the dual patrol had gone on for half an hour—the little gang marching and whistling alongside, until they were almost rubbing shoulders with her—she felt it was time to do something. They all looked rather alike, black-avised with dark, dangling, dirty locks to match, but she turned to the one who seemed to be the leader, and said, 'Come in here, there's something I want to say to you.'

She led the way from the kennels to her sitting-room, her library, only a few yards distant, a limb of the main body of the house.

They followed her in and stood around her, with the same look, between half-closed eyes, suggesting something they would like to do, if they could decide on it.

Nerina didn't ask them to sit down; she stood in their midst, and looked up at them.

'Now,' she said, as briskly as she could, 'There's something I want to ask you. Why are you here? What is all this about?'

A shuffling of feet; an exchange of interrogative looks; and their spokesman said,

'It's the spirit of adventure, I suppose.'

'You call it the spirit of adventure,' said Nerina. '*I* should call it something else.'

And for several minutes she told them, looking up from one face to another, for they were all big boys, what *she* would call it.

When she had finished her tirade she nodded a dismissal, and the little gang, rather sheepishly, filed out, no more to be seen.

*

Not long afterwards the vet turned up. 'I'm sorry, Miss Willough-by,' he said, 'but those damned birds took longer than I thought. And it was just as I expected—one of the cobs had done the other in—he was lying down on the grass with his neck and his head stretched out and his eyes glazing. I gave him an injection as quick as I could, but I'm afraid it was too late—I didn't hear any swan-song—and I gave the other a boot, which I hope he will remember. The lady in the case was standing by, looking more coy than you can believe, so I gave her a boot too, just to teach her. I suppose they can't help the way they behave, but it is annoying, to be called out as early as that—just for swans, because they are, or some of them are, said to be, the Queen's birds. And they are nearly the only birds, besides cocks and fighting-cocks, and birds of prey, which set out to kill each other. Sparrows have their squabbles but they are soon over, and I wouldn't get out of bed to separate *them*. Now what can I do for you, Miss Willoughby?'

Nerina explained, and together they inspected the suffering occupants of the kennels. No need to tell—it was abundantly evident on the floor of their well-kept abodes—what was the matter with them. But was it a symptom or a cause?

'I'm sure you've done right,' the vet said. 'It's one of those unexplained epidemics that dogs, even more than human beings, are liable to. But you might also give them these,' and he brought out from his bag a bottle of pills. He frowned. 'One never knows, in this kind of thing, if it's better to let Nature take its course. Don't hesitate to call me if they aren't improving. I hope that by tomorrow *all* the swans in England will be dead.'

He waved and drove away.

*

Having administered his pills to the afflicted animals, some of whom were willing to swallow them and some not, Nerina went back to her library sitting-room, and sat down to answer some letters that had been too long unanswered.

It was now eleven o'clock; the traditional hour of respite and relaxation. She might well have felt tired but she didn't, for work was more of a stimulus to her than leisure, or pleasure.

Presently, while her fingers were still busy on the writing-paper, a daily help came in with a tray, on which was some of the household silver, that was cleaned once a week.

'May I have your clock, Miss Nerina?'

'Yes, of course,' said Nerina, nodding towards the chimney-piece where it stood, and the clock went away with the salt-cellars, pepper-pots, spoons and the rest of the silver-ware which Nerina, who was not much interested in such matters, thought it necessary to keep bright and shining.

The clock—the little, silver travelling-clock, had been a present, and she was fond of it. It was engraved, on the margin,

'For Nerina, from a friend.' It didn't say who the friend was, which made Nerina all the more aware of who it was.

She went on writing, always with an ear for sounds from the kennels, and didn't notice the passing of time, until she was suddenly startled by the pealing of the front-door bell, which, clanging in the kitchen, also resounded through the house.

Was there anyone to answer it, apart from the cook, who never answered the door if she could help it? Yes, there was Hilda, the silver-polisher, who didn't leave till after lunch.

Nerina settled down to her correspondence, but was disturbed by another, louder peal.

'Oh dear, must I go?' she asked herself, for she was more tired than she knew.

A third peal, and then silence, silence for what seemed quite a long time.

Nerina was licking the last envelope, and preparing to go out to see how the dogs were getting on, when Hilda came in.

'Excuse me, Miss Nerina,' she said, 'but something has happened.'

'Oh, what?' asked Nerina. She was not specially observant, and was obsessed by the thought of what might be happening in the kennels, but she saw that Hilda had a white face.

'It's the clock, Miss Nerina, your little clock.'

'What about it?'

'It's disappeared.'

Nerina got up from her desk. How many times, during the day, had her thoughts been violently switched from one subject to another.

'Disappeared?'

'Yes, Miss Nerina, I had it on the tray, ready to clean, and the door-bell rang, twice, no three times, when I was having my elevenses, and a boy was at the front door with a parcel. I told him where to put the parcel—groceries or something—in the pantry, and went back to the kitchen, to finish my cup of tea, and when I went back to the pantry, it was gone.'

'The clock, you mean?'

'Yes, Miss Nerina. None of us would have taken it, as you well know.'

Nerina did know. For a few minutes the loss of the clock, that symbol of an ancient friendship, which had faithfully told her the time of day in many places, and for many years, brought tears to her eyes.

'Never mind, Hilda,' she said, 'We shall get over it. Worse things happen at sea,' and she went out to look at the dogs, who were ill—which the clock, whatever might have been its fate, was not.

*

The next morning the dogs were clearly on the mend. Nerina and the kennel-maid, who was now recovered, between them cleaned out the grosser relics of the dogs' indisposition. Nerina was not usually time-conscious, but when she went back, after washing, to her sitting-room—a spy-hole on the dogs—the clock wasn't there, and the claims of human, as distinct from canine friend-ship, began to assert themselves.

When she had looked round for the tenth time, to see what hour it was, Hilda appeared.

'There's a young gentleman to see you, Miss Nerina.'

'A young gentleman? Who is he?'

'I couldn't catch his name, Miss Nerina. He speaks that rough.'

'Where is he?'

'In the hall, the outer hall. I didn't want him to come any nearer, because I think he's the same young man as came in yesterday, when you lost your clock.'

Nerina got up and went through another room into the hall.

There was a young man, who looked so like the other members of the group of youths who had (so to speak) dogged her footsteps yesterday, that she couldn't tell whether he was one of them or not.

'What do you want?' she asked him, rather curtly.

'It's like this, madam,' he said, and produced from his pocket her little silver clock. 'I found this on the drive leading to your house, and as it has your name on it, and your birthday,' he added, giving it another look, 'I thought you might value it, so I brought it back.'

She took the clock from his outstretched palm, which remained outstretched, as though for a reward; and slightly shook her head.

'I'm glad you brought it back,' she said. 'It makes things better for everyone, doesn't it?'

He didn't answer, and at once took his leave.

FALL IN AT THE DOUBLE

PHILIP OSGOOD had bought his house in the West Country soon after the Second World War, in the year 1946 to be exact. It had the great merit, for him, of being on the river—a usually slow-flowing stream, but deep, and liable to sudden sensational rises in height, eight feet in as many hours, which flooded the garden but could not reach the house. The house was fairly large, mainly Regency, with earlier and later additions; it had encountered the floods of many years without being washed away; so when he saw the water invading the garden, submerging the garden wall and even overflowing the lawn (on which swans sometimes floated), he didn't feel unduly worried, for the house stood on a hillock which was outside flood-range.

Philip had always liked the house, chiefly because of its situation, its long view over the meadows, and because it had, in one corner of the garden, a boat-house, and rowing was his favourite pastime. He sometimes asked his visitors, who were not many (for who can entertain guests nowadays?) to go out with him in the boat, a cockly affair, known technically as a 'sculling gig', with a sliding seat. It could take one passenger, but this passenger had to sit absolutely still—not a foot this way or that, hardly a head-shake—or the boat would tip over.

Moreover, besides its natural instability, it took in water at an alarming rate, so that the passenger—he or she—found himself ankle-deep in water, though doing his best to look as if he were enjoying it. The landscape through which the river ambled, or flowed, or hastened, was perfectly beautiful, and this was Philip's excuse (besides mere selfishness) for beguiling his friends into the boat.

The day came when this treacherous vessel (happily with no other occupant in it) overturned, and Philip found himself in the water. Being a practised, though not a good swimmer, he was not unduly disturbed. Although it was March and the water was cold —and he was wearing his leather jacket and the rest of his polar outfit—he thought: 'I will get hold of the boat and tow it back to the boat-house.'

Alas, he had reckoned without the current, swollen by recent rains, and he found that far from his towing the boat back to the boat-house, it was towing him down-river to the weir, where who knew what might not happen?

He at once relinquished the boat to its fate and after a struggle —for he was too old for this sort of thing—he reached the boat-house, the only possible landing-place, for everywhere else the banks were too high and steep, and he went dripping up to his bedroom.

It so happened that this very day he had engaged a new facto-tum, who was to cook and drive for him. His job with Philip was his first job of this kind—he had had others—and it was his first night in Philip's house. His room faced Philip's, an arrangement Philip was glad of, for being an elderly hypochondriac, he liked to have someone within call.

Nothing came of the river-episode—no pneumonia, no bron-chitis—not at least for the moment—but who could tell? And suddenly he wondered if the house, which had seemed so wel-coming and friendly over twenty years, had something against him?

*

The next morning, when the new factotum called him at eight o'clock with a pot of tea, he asked, just as a routine inquiry.

'How did you sleep last night, Alfred?'

'Oh,' said Alfred who, like so many gentlemen's gentlemen, when they still exist, had been in the Services, 'I didn't sleep a wink, sir.' He sounded quite cheerful.

Philip, who himself suffered from insomnia, was distressed.

'I hope your bed was comfortable?'

'Oh yes, sir, couldn't have been more comfortable.'

'I'm glad of that. But perhaps you are one of the people—I am one myself—who don't sleep well in a strange bed?'

'Oh no, sir, I sleep like a log. I could sleep anywhere, on a clothes-line with a marlin-spike for a pillow.'

Philip didn't know what a marlin-spike was, but as an aid to rest it didn't sound very helpful.

'I'm so sorry,' he said, baffled. 'Then what was it that kept you awake?'

'It was the noises, sir.'

Philip sat up in bed and automatically began to listen for noises but there were none. One side of the house faced the main road where there was plenty of noise by day, and some by night; the other side, on which his bedroom lay, overlooked the long broad meadow, skirted, at no great distance, by the main railway line from London. Philip, in his sleepless hours, was used to the passing of nocturnal trains: indeed they soothed him rather than otherwise. There was the one-fifty, the two-twenty, and the three-forty-five; he didn't resent them, he rather welcomed them, as establishing his identity with the outside world.

Alfred was standing by his bed, tea-pot in hand.

'Shall I pour out for you, sir?'

'Yes, please, Alfred. But what did you mean by noises?'

Alfred began to pour the tea into his cup.

'Oh, just noises, sir, just noises.'

Alfred (Alf to his friends) handed Philip his bed-jacket.

'But what sort of noises?'

'Oh, I couldn't quite describe, sir. First there was a pattering of feet on the staircase, really quite loud, and then I heard a voice say, like a sergeant-major's—very autocratic, if you know what I mean—"Fall in at the double, fall in at the double, fall in at the double."'

'And what happened then?'

'Nothing much happened. The footsteps stopped, and a sort of smell—a weedy sort of smell—came into the room. I didn't pay much attention to it, and then I went to sleep.'

*

Thinking this over, Philip was puzzled. Could Alfred, or Alf, have possibly known that the house had been occupied by the Army during the war—the Second World War? There were people who could have told him—the gardener and his wife who lived up-stairs could have told him, supposing they knew; but would they have had time to tell him, in the few short hours since his arrival?

But there it was—the tramping of footsteps down the un-carpeted staircase (for it would have been uncarpeted during the Army's occupation), the thrice-repeated command, 'Fall in at the double'—what did it mean?

And then this weedy smell?

*

Philip couldn't sleep the next night, and expected to be told that Alfred couldn't sleep either; but when Alfred called him with a bright morning face, and Philip asked him if he had had a good night or a better night, he answered promptly, and as if surprised: 'Oh yes, sir, I slept like a log.'

Philip was glad to hear this, but something—a suggestion, a muttering from his subconscious mind—still irked him. He knew that certain people—people in the village and outside—had cer-tain reservations about his house. What they were he didn't know, and naturally, they didn't tell him; only a faint accent of doubt—as if referring to some rather shady acquaintance—coloured their voices when they spoke of it. But when he asked a friend of his who owned a much larger and grander house, if he thought his riverside abode might be haunted, his friend replied, 'Oh Philip, but is it *old* enough?'

Philip was slightly offended. It was a vulgar error to think a ghost needed a long pedigree. His house was quite old enough to be haunted; and this recent visitation, if it was one, had nothing to do with the house's age as a resort for ghosts.

He was not unduly superstitious but there was a nerve in him that vibrated to supernatural fears, and though he tried to calm them during the following days, by the reflection that he had lived in the house for over twenty years without any trouble other than the normal troubles—burst pipes, gas escapes, failures of electricity and so on, that are the lot of many old and decaying houses—he didn't feel so comfortable, so at home with his home, with his thoughts as he used to be.

Supposing?

But was there anything, abstract or concrete, spiritual or material, to suppose?

Alfred professed to be psychic, and familiar with poltergeists and other familiars (Philip laughed to himself, rather half-heartedly, at this mental joke), otherwise he wouldn't have taken the manifestations on the staircase so lightly; but that didn't explain why they had such an obvious bearing on the recent history of the house.

Forget about it, forget about it, and Philip had almost forgotten about it when, a few nights later, he was awakened by a thunderous knock on his bedroom door, three times repeated. It was the loudest sound he had ever heard; the footsteps of the Commendatore coming up the staircase in *Don Giovanni*, were nothing like as loud.

'Come in!' he shouted, unaware of the time, and almost unaware, having taken a sleeping pill, where he himself was. 'Come in!' he shouted again, thinking that perhaps it was Alfred with his early morning tea.

But no one came; and it couldn't have been Alfred, for when he looked at his watch, it was five o'clock in the morning.

Turning over in bed, he tried to go to sleep; but his subconscious mind had taken alarm and wouldn't let him; and he lay awake listening for another summons until three hours later, when a much gentler, hardly audible knock, that didn't even expect an answer, announced Alfred with Philip's early morning tea.

Philip turned a tired, sleep-deprived face towards him.

'Did you have a good night, Alfred?'

'Oh yes, sir, pretty good. A few noises, you know.'

'You didn't hear a terrific hammering on my door' (Alfred's bedroom door was only an arm's length from Philip's) 'about five o'clock this morning?'

'Oh no, sir, nothing like that. A few scurrying noises, could have been rats.'

Philip, with lack-lustre eyes, sipped his tea. Could he have *imagined* the knocking? No, it was much too loud. But could it have been a sound heard in a dream—the tail-end of a dream? Philip hadn't had many dreams of late years. Sleeping-pills inhibited them; that was one of their side-effects, and a bad one, for dreams were an outlet for the subconscious mind, and if denied this outlook, it took its revenge in other ways. In madness, perhaps? One *saw* things in dreams of course and one was aware of conversations; but were these conversations conveyed by sound, or by the illusion of the dream? As far as his recollections went, communication in dreams went by sight, and by some telepathic process, and not by sound—certainly not by such sounds as the four tremendous thumps which had awakened him.

So convinced was he of their material reality that while he was dressing he opened his bedroom door, and examined its other side, fully expecting to see marks on it which might have been made by a sledge-hammer. There were none; the off-white paint was as smooth and undented as it had always been. To make assurance doubly sure, he held the door open, where the light could catch it at different angles; and then he saw something which in all his twenty-odd years of opening the door, he had never seen.

Beneath its coating of thick paint, something was written, printed rather. White over white, very hard to decipher, but at last he made it out:

PRIVATE

LIEUT.-COLONEL ALEXANDER McCREETH

Well, that explained itself. Lieut.-Col. McCreeth had occupied Philip's bedroom.

Sometime during the war years he may have used it as an orderly-room, a sitting-room, or a bedroom, but when using it he didn't want to be disturbed. Was the repeated rat-tat-tat meant to disturb his privacy, perhaps for military reasons? The previous owners of the house, who had occupied it for a year or two after the Army left, had redecorated it, and tried to wipe out all trace of their military predecessors. They must have spent a lot of money on it, and then gone away, quite ready to go, apparently, for they had sold it to Philip at a reasonable price. No haggling. Why?

It was years since he had seen the vendors and he didn't even know their whereabouts. And if he had, what could he ask them?

He began to entertain absurd fancies, such as that it was he who had been ordered to fall in at the double and the mysterious knocking was meant to awaken him to the urgency of some military exercise, for which he would otherwise be late. Perhaps the safety of the country depended on it. Perhaps an invasion was imminent?

Not now, of course, but then.

Gradually these fancies began to wear off, and only showed themselves in an almost invincible reluctance, on Philip's part, to ask Alfred if he had had any more psychic experience. At last, when all seemed set fair, he put the question.

'Oh yes, sir, often. But I didn't want to tell you, because I thought it might bother you.'

Philip's heart sank.

'What sort of things?'

'Well, nothing that I've heard myself, except those noises I've told you about, and the voice saying "Fall in at the double!" But anything may happen in an old house like this.'

'But you haven't heard anything else?'

'As a matter of fact I have, sir, but it's only gossip, things they natter about at the local. Places like this, so far from civilization, they haven't much to talk about.'

'Tell me what it was.'

'May I sit down, sir?'

Alfred sat down, bent forward to get his shirt-cuffs into the correct position, leaned back and said:

'Well, it was about this Colonel.'

'You mean Colonel McCreeth?'

'Yes, Colonel McCreeth. They couldn't pronounce his name properly—they're uneducated here. But they said he was unpopular with the other men who were living here, in this house I mean, at the time. He was a dictatorial type, like some of them are, and they had it in for him. He used to get them up from bed when it wasn't a bit necessary, just to look at the moon, so to say, pretending there was an air raid, when there wasn't. And so they got fed up.'

'I don't wonder. And then?'

'Well, he picked on a certain bloke who had said or done something out of turn and gave him C.B.—this house counted as a barracks, I believe—and this bloke, and three or four others, slept in my room—you may remember how it was in the Army, sir, they didn't always pay much attention to the comfort of the men.'

'Yes, I do remember,' Philip said.

'Well, this fellow was a sort of trouble-maker, and he had it in for the Colonel, who wasn't liked by any of them, and he got their sergeant, who didn't like him either, to make a sort of plot. Very wrong of them, of course, and against discipline, but you can't try people, even soldiers, beyond a certain point.'

'Of course not.'

'So, as I was saying, they put their heads together, and ran downstairs, saying "Fall in at the double", and the sergeant knocked at the Colonel's door—your door, sir—and he came out in his pyjamas—and said, "What the hell is this?" And the Sergeant said, "It's someone down by the river, sir. He's acting very suspicious. We think he may be a German spy." The Colonel cursed, but he got into his coat and trousers—it was a cold night—and went with them—about three dozen of them—down to the river bank. And what happened afterwards no one seemed to know. You know what men are like when they get angry and excited. It spreads from one to another—a dozen men would do what one man wouldn't—and the Colonel was a heavy drinker— but anyhow the upshot was he fell into the river, and was found drowned at the weir below your house. The river was low, so he wasn't carried over it.'

'Dear me,' said Philip, though a stronger expression would have suited his feelings better. 'Do you think any of this is true?'

Alfred smiled and shrugged his shoulders. 'They're that uneducated in these parts.'

*

A few nights later at the same hour as before, five o'clock, Philip was awakened by a knocking at his door. 'Come in!' he shouted, still fuddled with sleep, and still unaware if he was awake or dreaming, 'Come in!' he repeated, and it was then he heard the thrice-given order, 'Fall in at the double, fall in at the double, fall in at the double,' followed by the clatter of heavy footsteps on the bare boards of the staircase.

So intent was he on listening to this that he didn't see his bedroom door open—it may have opened of itself as it sometimes did when not securely latched—but at any rate it was open, as he could tell from the moonlight from the hall window, above the staircase, struggling into the densely curtained room. Faint as it was, the moonlight showed him that someone had come in when the door opened, for he could dimly descry the head and the back of a tall man, edging his way round Philip's bed, apparently looking for something. It was more like a presence than a person, a movement than a man, the footsteps made no sound on the thick carpet, but it seemed to stop in front of the wardrobe, and fumble there.

A burglar? If it was a burglar, and if all he wanted was a few clothes, well and good; he might be armed, and Philip was in no state to resist an armed man. Some said—the police even said— that in certain cases, in this age of violence, it was safer not to 'have a go' at a man who might be desperate.

The telephone was at his left hand, the switch of the bedside lamp at his right: yet he dared not use either, he dared not even stir, lest the intruder should realize he was awake.

After what seemed an unconscionable time, he heard or thought he heard, sounds of groping in the recesses of the wardrobe. This activity, whatever it was, ceased and a silence followed which Philip took to mean that the burglar (for who else could he be?) had finished his search and was taking himself off. Philip pressed the back of his head against the pillow and shut his eyes, for the man was now coming towards him, face forwards. But Philip's pretence of sleep hadn't deceived him; he stopped and peered down at him. Philip's eyes opened: they couldn't help themselves, and he saw the stranger's face. Mask-like, the indistinct features kept their own secret, but their colour was the colour of the moonlight on them. Drawing nearer, stooping closer, outside the moonlight's ray, they were invisible; but a voice which must have come through the unseen lips, though the whole body seemed to utter it, said:

'Fall in and follow me. At the double, mind you, at the double,' and a shadow, momentarily blotting out the moonbeams, slid through the doorway.

Seized by an irresistible inner compulsion, Philip jumped out of bed and without waiting to put a coat over his pyjamas, or slippers on his feet, followed the visitant downstairs in a direction he knew as well as if it had been directed to him by a radar beam.

On the wall that separated the garden from the river he saw first of all a line of heads, he couldn't tell how many, wearing Army caps, turning this way and that, bobbing and nudging, and heard an angry buzz of talk, as of bees, whose hive is threatened. At the sign of his precursor, only a few yards ahead of him, silence fell, and they drew apart, leaving a gap between them in the shallow river-wall. But they were still leaning towards each other, some of their faces and silhouettes moonstruck, the rest in darkness.

'Now, boys, what is all this?' asked their Colonel, for he it must have been, in a cheerful, would-be rallying tone. 'Why have you got me up at this time of night? There isn't an air raid.' And his moonlit face, revolving slowly in its lunar circuit, scanned the night sky.

'No sir, you know what it is,' said a voice, a low, level voice charged with menace. 'We're fed up with you, that's what it is.'

They were beginning to close in on him, their hands were already round his legs, when he called out, 'You've done this before. Take him, he's my double!' And he pointed to Philip, shivering behind him on the lawn.

'Shall we, Jack? Shall we, Bill? He's one of them, we might as well.'

Their strong hands were round him and Philip, hardly struggling, felt himself being hoisted over the garden wall, to where, a few feet below, he could see his own face mirrored in the water.

'Let's get rid of the bastard!'

*

The next thing Philip knew was a hand on his shoulder, and he heard another voice, saying:

'Good God, sir, what are you doing here? You might catch your death of cold.'

He couldn't speak while Alfred was helping him over the wall.

'Thank you, thank you,' he gasped, when he had got his breath back. 'I might have been drowned if it hadn't been for you. But where are the others?'

He looked back at the depopulated garden wall, no dark heads bobbing and whispering, neck to neck, no limbs bracing themselves for violence; only the moon shining as innocently as that de-virginated satellite can shine.

'But how did you *know*?'

'I have my ways of finding out,' said Alfred darkly. 'A hot bath, a hot bottle, a whisky perhaps, and then bed for you, sir. And don't pay any attention to that lot, they're up to no good.'

THE PRAYER

ANTHONY EASTERFIELD was not really religious, unless the word 'religious' is capable of the widest and vaguest interpretation, but he was religious to the extent of not being a materialist. He was sure he was not a materialist, and if the word was mentioned in his presence, or if he came across it in a book, or if it occurred to his mind unbidden (as words will), he at once chased it away. Materialist indeed! Perish the thought! The human race was dying of materialism. Better a drunkard's death which did at any rate result from some form of spirit.

At the same time he was aware that many of the phenomena of which he specially disapproved, 'the worship of the motor-car', for instance, had a relish of spirit, if not of salvation in it, besides the petrol to which motorists were addicted, for in one sense they were alcoholics all.

He himself had a car, and a man to drive it—for Anthony couldn't drive, and he knew, from mortifying efforts to pass the driving test, that it was much better for himself and everybody else that he shouldn't try to.

The car was a convenience to him, but to his driver it was much more than a convenience, it was an emblem of religion. His driver was not satisfied with it, or with its performance in many, if not in all, directions—as many people are dissatisfied with their religions (if any), feeling that their religions have let them down. Anthony's car had often let Copperthwaite down, and it was anything but the status-symbol that he coveted; at the same time the creed of automobilism was in his blood, and nothing could eradicate it.

'What you really want, sir,' (on a special occasion he would deign to call Anthony 'Sir' though he would more willingly have addressed the car as such) 'is a car with a prestige value.'

(The fact that Anthony did not and never would 'want' such a car never penetrated Copperthwaite's car-intoxicated consciousness.)

'Now the Roland-Rex 1967,' he went on, trying to make the arcana of automobilism clear to Anthony's non-mechanical mind, 'with over-drive, under-drive, self-drive, automatic gears, et cetera, is just the car for you. It is a splendid car. I could tell you more about its performance, only you wouldn't be interested, but its prestige value is enormous. I doubt if even a Rolls-Royce—'

Anthony Easterfield was indifferent, or nearly indifferent, to the prestige value of a Roland-Rex, but he knew that Copperthwaite's interest in it, besides being mechanical, was also snobbish, and snobbism implies a sense of values that is not simply materialistic, even if it could scarcely be called spiritual.

To make people stare! To watch them gather round the Roland-Rex, wide-eyed with admiration, exclaiming to each other, patting and stroking it if they dared—venerating it as an object of excellence. To surpass, to excel! Not to keep up with the Jones's but to leave them behind, scattering and gaping. The *deus ex machina*! The God in the car!

Copperthwaite spent hours, literally hours, on Anthony's commonplace little car, making it shine so that you could see your face in it; and when its lower quarters went wrong, as they often did, he would be under it with outstretched legs, and his face, if it were visible, which it seldom was, wearing a beatific expression, as if at last he had found true happiness. And if Anthony called him to come out of his dark grimy, oily hiding-place into the light of day, he would look disappointed, and almost cross, as if his orisons had been interrupted.

Laborare est orare. Copperthwaite's happy (although to Anthony), his unenviable labours, were a form of prayer to the *deus ex machina*, the god in the car. If only he could save up enough to buy a Roland-Rex! Then Copperthwaite's dream would come true, and if his labours were doubled, so would his prayers be. To be prostrate under the chassis of a Roland-Rex! To feel its oil dripping gently on his face! To be in close touch with its genitals (excuse the phrase) what bliss! What more could a man want? To labour for, and by so doing, to pray to the embodied principle of mechanical engineering! To communicate with it (no levity intended) by the oil dripping from it—to be at one with it! Anthony envied Copperthwaite his instinctive identification with the object of his devotion, his conviction that it was more important than he was, and that in its service was perfect freedom.

Anthony had learned to recognize a Roland-Rex, for when they passed, or, as seldom happened, overtook one, Copperthwaite would draw his attention to it. 'Now that's what we ought to have, sir.'

Anthony, who wanted Copperthwaite to be happy, would groan inwardly and think about his bank-balance.

He realized that Copperthwaite's passion for cars was of a religious nature, and respected him for it, for he too, was religious after a fashion, although it was a different fashion from Copperthwaites.

Laborare est orare. To work is to pray. Yes; but is the converse true? *Orare est laborare?*—to pray is to work? It may be; many people besides the Saints had wrestled in prayer. Sweat had poured off their foreheads, tears had run down their cheeks; they had thrown their bodies this way and that; they had been taken up unconscious for dead. All this due to the physical effort of prayer. Labour! Could anyone labour more than that? Copperthwaite certainly laboured in his unuttered prayer to Anthony's car; he withdrew himself from the light of day, he put himself into the most uncomfortable positions the body could assume, while studying and communing with the object of his adoration—albeit with its baser parts. His communication with it was immediate and instinctive, and needed no effort on his part; he required no confirmation from the car to assure him that he was completely *en rapport* with it, and it with him. Labour thrown away! No fear; even if he couldn't find out what was wrong, the attempt

to do so was its own reward. Another time, another hour or
two, with his back on the cement and his eyes on a jungle of pipes
(what he actually saw that so captivated him, Anthony, who was
totally devoid of mechanical sense, never knew), he would find
out, and his loving identification with the car would be closer
than ever.

As for being brought out unconscious! Copperthwaite never
looked more alive and kicking (for he had more or less to kick
himself out) than when he emerged from under the car, patted
its bonnet and gave it a grateful and a loving look.

Anthony's orisons were physically much less laborious, for they
only involved kneeling and sometimes wriggling and pressing his
forehead against the bed, or the chair, or the pew, or wherever he
happened to find convenient for his devotions. He didn't go to
church much; he knew, or had known, the order of the service so
well that he listened to it with only half an ear; he preferred
private to public worship. Following its majestic sequence did
not give him time to slip in his own petitions. These needed an
effort of memory which he could not compass while the clergy-
man, the choir, or the congregation, were all shouting or muttering against it. His prayers needed constant modification; this or
that person had to be left out, this or that person put in. The task
of selection and discrimination was difficult; and to perform it,
Anthony felt he must be alone with God, undisturbed by the
traffic noises, and the traffic signals, red, yellow, and green, on
the Road to Heaven.

But did he really believe in the efficacy of his prayers? Did he
really believe they would be answered? Did he believe in God, as
implicitly and explicitly, as Copperthwaite believed in his car?
Or was it all a superstition on his part, a sort of insurance against
some calamity that might befall his friends or himself? or, having
forgotten to mention this or that desired benefit, to have deprived
them, and him, of some happiness?

He put his friends first, because he had had doubts about the
propriety of praying for himself; perhaps for oneself one could
only ask God to forgive one's sins? To ask him to forgive other

people's sins was an impertinence, an almost blasphemous
prompting of God's Will, that Anthony would never be guilty of.
Some of his friends were quite bad, and urgently in need of
divine, moral and spiritual aid, so Anthony never presumed to
mention who they were or how they could be improved.

His prayers, however, did include a long string of names of
friends for whom he made a general, and sometimes an individual
petition. They were divided mainly into two groups: friends who
were still living, and relations of friends who had died. Anthony
never counted them up (he had a Biblical distrust of counting the
numbers of people) but together they must have come to forty at
least. As he murmured the name, its owner for a moment came
back to him, each one, living or dead, a link in the chain of his
life, a link of love, a continuation of his own personality, a proof
of identity, his and theirs.

But there are always snags, even in prayers. Anthony did not
offer prayers for the dead. Not for doctrinal reasons, but because
he thought he could do nothing for them; they were in the hands
of God. But he prayed for the comfort and consolations of their
relations, and friends, even when he knew that their relations
and friends were quite glad to see the last of them.

The list of these relations and friends grew longer and longer,
as, one after another, from love's shining circle the gems dropped
away. A queue formed; and Anthony, in self-defence, had to omit
certain names in order to make room for others, just as, in the
cemetery of San Michele in Venice, the bodies of the dead are
only allowed a few years of earthly habitation before they are
turned out. Without having to accuse himself of favouritism,
Anthony had to decide whose relations were in the greater need
of his prayers, who should stay and who should go.

There was another thing. Some of Anthony's friends whom,
living, he had prayed for, had before they died and passed out of
the land of the living, changed their names, owing to divorce, re-
marriage, titles for themselves or their husbands. Would God
know the original 'Mary' of his prayers for the living, for the
Mrs. X, or the Lady X, for whose bereaved relations Anthony

asked God for sympathy? Anthony knew how absurd this question was. God was no student of Who's Who or Debrett; he would know who Mary was; but just as in ordinary conversation one has to explain who 'Mary' may be, so, in Anthony's appeals to the Deity, he felt he ought to explain who this 'Mary' was. God was no respecter of persons; but Anthony felt he should take the trouble to differentiate this Mary from the other Marys, one of whom had been the mother of Christ.

Another thing that made praying laborious was that in this long list of names he might have left out someone. Every religion has its ritual which must be strictly observed; a small fault, a casual omission, may invalidate the whole proceedings. Anthony knew his prayers by heart, and wasn't ashamed of rattling them off at high speed so long as he gave a flick of affection to each name, alive or dead, for whom he prayed. But sometimes he had the feeling that one name—just one—had escaped him. And then he must start all over again, and sometimes twice, to make sure that no one had been omitted. Apart from the effort of repetition, he didn't like doing this; he felt it smacked of conscience, not of devotion, but all the same, he had to.

His prayers for the living, who had not been bereaved, but were perhaps sad, and ill, and unfortunate, were easier, because he felt that for them his intercessions were the living word of encouragement, and not the dead word of condolence. For them he did not have to pray for the negative blessings, if negative they were, of consolation and comfort; he could pray for their future happiness (if not, of course, based on some improper relationship), the success of their undertakings, their personal, general and material welfare. There was nothing wrong in this. The Old Testament had condemned many, indeed most things, but not the ideal of prosperity. Prosperity had been taken from Job: it was indeed the *gravamen* of his spiritual suffering. But in the end it had been restored to him ten-fold.

So Anthony did not feel it was irreligious to wish for his friends, not too much burdened and borne down by sorrow, the desire of their hearts, even in the material sphere. Did not devout

Roman Catholics pray to St. Anthony, his namesake, for the recovery of some unimportant object, a wrist-watch, for instance, which they had lost? One could not, oneself, pray to God for the recovery of a wrist-watch; in relation to God it would be outside one's terms of reference; and, as a Protestant, one did not pray to the Saints. But on behalf of someone else, one might, and that was how Anthony came to pray that Copperthwaite, to whom he was much attached, might be granted the gift of a Roland-Rex motor-car. He did not think of himself as concerned in the gift: he only wanted it for Copperthwaite.

*

Rising stiffly from his knees, after an unusually long and laborious session of intercession, he felt he *might* have done someone a good turn. It is difficult to know what a friend really wants; and what will be good for him if he wants it. Copperthwaite wanted a Roland-Rex.

*

A few days later Copperthwaite came to him with a rather stiff face and said,

'I'm afraid, sir, I shall have to ask for my cards.'

Copperthwaite had been with Anthony for a good many years, and the phrase was unfamiliar to him.

'Your cards, what cards, Copperthwaite?' He thought they might be some sort of playing cards.

'My cards, sir, my stamps and my P.A.Y.E., same as you have always paid for.'

'You can have them, of course,' said Anthony, bewildered. 'That is, if I can find them. But what do you want them for?'

Copperthwaite's face stiffened yet more: Anthony could hardly recognize him.

'Because I've been offered a better job sir, if you'll excuse me saying so. I've been happy with you, sir, and you mustn't think I don't appreciate what you have done for me. But a man in my position has to look after himself—you might not understand that, sir, being a gentleman.'

'I don't understand,' said Anthony, still bewildered.

Copperthwaite's face grew stiffer.

'An American gentleman—no offence to you, sir—has asked me to go to him. The porter in this block of flats told him about me. He pays very good money.'

'I can raise your salary, if you like,' said Anthony, his own face beginning to stiffen.

'Oh no, sir, I couldn't ask you to do that, I'm not a gold-digger, and besides—'

'Besides what?' asked Anthony crossly.

'Besides, he has a Roland-Rex car, and it's always been my ambition to drive one, as you know, sir.'

'When do you want to go?' asked Anthony.

'A week next Saturday. That will give you time to find another man.'

'I'm not sure it will,' said Anthony. 'But meanwhile I'll look for your cards.'

*

The week passed, and Anthony tried in vain to find a replacement for Copperthwaite. In answer to his advertisement, several candidates for the job presented themselves and interviews were arranged. He was on his best behaviour, and they were on their best behaviour; who could tell? 'There is no art,' as Shakespeare, or his spokesman, truly said, 'to find the mind's construction in the face.' As for references, so his friends assured him, they were often written by the applicants themselves. 'Mr. Anthony Bragshaw' (surprising how many of them were called by his own name) 'is honest, sober, and trustworthy: a good driver, and an excellent plain cook. I have no hesitation whatever in recommending him for the situation he is applying for.'

Two or three of these replies were written on the writing-paper, and contained the telephone number of the applicant's employer: but when he rang up the number, he did not get a reply.

Anthony himself could not cook, nor could he drive: pushing

up the seventies, he needed outside help. Meals were not so difficult; he could go out for food. And as for transport, there were buses, and tubes and taxis, if one could find a taxi at the right moment. It was ridiculous to complain of things which, as Sir Thomas Browne said, 'all the world doth suffer from' (including death).

He didn't know what to do with his car, so he left it in the communal garage, where it had a place, 5A. Sometimes, when he engaged one of the porters, or a casual man to drive it, it was neither found in 5A, nor returned to 5A. Someone else had been taking it for a ride.

Copperthwaite himself Anthony saw, from time to time, for his employer lived on the opposite side of the Square, in one of the few houses that hadn't been 'converted' into flats. Anthony didn't always recognize him, for Copperthwaite had been so smartened up. He wore the conventional chauffeur's uniform, blue suit, black tie, peak cap—and he looked straight ahead of him, as if other cars were in the way (as they often were).

He and Anthony used sometimes to exchange distant greetings in which the condescension (if there is a condescension in greetings) was always on Copperthwaite's side. And indeed the Roland-Rex was a sight to dream of, not to tell. At least Anthony, with his ignorance of all that made one car superior to another, couldn't have told! But he did at least realize that here was a car that from its sheer bulk, more noticeable behind than before, as if it wore a bustle, took up half the street.

Copperthwaite did not always recognize Anthony when Anthony on foot, and Copperthwaite, eyes half-closed, installed in his Roland-Rex fortress, met each other. The smugness on Copperthwaite's dozing face was sometimes more than Anthony could stand.

He consoled himself with the thought that Copperthwaite was (to misquote Mrs. Hemans) a creature of inferior blood, a proud but child-like form.

All the more was he surprised when one morning he received a letter with no stamp on it, brought by hand.

Dear Sir, (it said)

I wish to inform you that I have now terminated my engagement with my present employer, Mr. Almeric Duke. It is not
on account of any disagreement with Mr. Duke, who has been
both generous and understanding, but I am not happy with the
conditions of my service, especially as regards the car. From
what I am told, I understand you have not found another man,
sir, to drive your car and minister to your comforts, and if you
will consider my application to take me back into the position
in which I was always happy, I shall be much obliged.

I am, sir,

Yours respectfully,

J. Copperthwaite.

Anthony studied this missive with mixed feelings. Copperthwaite had not treated him well. His daily help, who had been
with him a good many years, and had known one or two of Copperthwaite's quickly changing predecessors, once said to him,
'You're too easy-going with them, Mr. Easterfield, that's what it
is.' She did not mean it as a compliment. All very well and good;
but if Anthony wasn't easy-going with them, indeed if he criti-
cised them—their cooking, their driving, the friends of both
sexes, or any sex, that they brought into the flat from time to time,
their unwarrantable absences or their sometimes more disturbing
presences—at the faintest hint of criticism they departed, almost
before the offending words were out of his mouth. 'Easy-going'
on his part meant easy-going on theirs; but if he had adopted a
policy of 'hard-going', he trembled to think what the results
might have been.

It was the recollection of these fugitive characters that made
Anthony think more kindly of Copperthwaite. Copperthwaite had
treated him badly but he had at any rate given him a week's
notice; he hadn't just 'slung his hook' (to use an old-fashioned
expression), leaving the keys of the flat and the car-keys on the
table with a pencilled note to say he was 'fed up'.

No, during the years that he and Copperthwaite had been

together they had got on very well—not a 'misword' between them. His daily help, who was nothing if not censorious, may have thought that Anthony was too easy-going with Copperthwaite; but there was no occasion for hard feelings.

Never take a servant back again was the advice of our forebears. The word 'servant' was now out of date, it was archaic; it could never be used in polite or impolite society. A 'servant' was 'staff': even one 'servant' was 'staff'. One envisaged a bundle of staves, of fasces (infamous word) once used as a symbol of their office by Roman Lictors, and then by Mussolini.

Copperthwaite a staff? The staff of life? Thinking of the dreary days and weeks that had passed since his departure, thinking of his forerunners, so much less helpful and hopeful than he, looking to the future, which seemed to hold in store nothing more alluring than an Old People's Home, Anthony began to think more favourably of Copperthwaite's return.

In spite of his elder's advice not to take back a 'servant', what harm could Copperthwaite do if he came back? He could become more 'bossy', Anthony supposed; he had always been a bit bossy, he used to decide for Anthony many small problems of food, wine, and so on, that Anthony had been too tired, or too old, or too uninterested, to decide for himself.

The worst he could do was to leave, as he had just done; and Anthony had survived that, and no doubt would survive it again.

*

But why did Copperthwaite want to give up this much better-paid, much more glamorous job, with the American gentleman on the other side of the Square, with the Roland-Rex to give it added prestige value?

Dear Copperthwaite, (he wrote)

If you would like to come back here, please do. I have made some tentative enquiries for other Staff, but I haven't fixed up anything, so if you want to come back you are at liberty to, and of course I shall be pleased to see you.

My car is still in the garage. It hasn't been used much since you went away, and I expect various things will have gone wrong with it, the battery will have run down and the tyres will need pumping up, and the *oil*!—but you will know about this better than I do.

Please let me know when you are ready to return, so that I can answer the answers to my advertisements for another Staff.

Yours sincerely,

Anthony Easterfield.

Copperthwaite's reply came promptly.

'Will be with you on Monday, Sir.'

So he must have given in his notice to the American gentleman before he got Anthony's answer. Rather mortifying to know that Copperthwaite took it for granted he would be welcome back: but what a relief to know that the rhythm and routine of his life so dismally interrupted would be resumed.

Say nothing to begin with; make no comment; express no curiosity.

Such were some of Anthony's resolutions on the Saturday before Copperthwaite was due back on Monday morning. But, when the bell of the flat-door pealed at 8 a.m. on Sunday, he was taken by surprise. Who was this? What was this? The porter, telling him he had left a tap dripping, flooding the flat below. An urgent letter on Her Majesty's Service, demanding Income Tax? The postman—but the postman never rang the bell unless he was carrying some object (usually of evil import) too bulky to pass through the letter-box—and besides, the post didn't come on Sunday.

So pessimistic was Anthony's imagination that he could not think of any summons at eight o'clock in the morning that did not presage disaster or even doom. A mere burglar, with a sawn-off shot-gun or a blunt instrument would have been a relief compared with the horrors Anthony had begun to envisage.

Copperthwaite said, 'I came a bit early, sir, because I know that eight o'clock is about the time you like your tea.'

'Well, yes, I do,' said Anthony, putting all his previous thoughts into reverse. 'And I expect you want some tea too.'

'All in good time, sir, all in good time,' said Copperthwaite, 'but meanwhile may I dispose of these bits and pieces?'

The bits and pieces were two very heavy and expensive suit-cases, made of white leather. Anthony admired them and wondered how Copperthwaite had come by them: the American gentleman, no doubt. He even envied them although when full—when bulging, as they now were—he couldn't have carried them a yard.

'Well, you know where to go,' he said, laughing rather feebly, 'the first on the right. You won't find it changed—no one has had it since you were there. All the same,' he added suddenly, 'I think the bed—the mattress—ought to be aired. The bed-clothes—the sheets and blankets are all right. They're in the airing-cupboard.'

'Don't worry, sir,' said Copperthwaite, bending down to pick up his suit-cases, 'aired or not aired, it's the same to me.'

Strong as Copperthwaite was, forty-three, forty-five?—his features showed the strain as he stooped to lift the suit-cases.

Anthony went back to bed, with various emotions, of which relief was uppermost. It was against his routine to say prayers in the morning, but he made a short act of thanksgiving for the mercy just received. A few minutes later appeared Copperthwaite, tea-tray in hand. Wearing his service-jacket he looked so like his old self—his slightly Red-Indian self—that Anthony could hardly believe that he had been away three, four, how many weeks?

'A steak for lunch, sir?'

'No, Copperthwaite, not a steak. My teeth, my remaining teeth, aren't equal to a steak. A cutlet, perhaps.'

'Yes, sir, a nice, tender cutlet. And for this evening a nice bit of fish, a Dover sole, perhaps.'

'No, I think a lemon sole. They don't sit so heavily on one's tummy, and they're cheaper, too.'

'I meant a lemon sole,' said Copperthwaite.

'Did he?' thought Anthony, with his eyes bent on Copperthwaite's broad retreating back, and his blue-black hair, which he

kept short and trim, army-fashion. Does he remember my requirements automatically, or has he been thinking them up?

The sound of voices disturbed his cogitations. His daily help
had arrived. 'So you're back?' he heard her say, 'like the bad
penny, who always turns up.' Anthony jumped out of bed and
shut the door which Copperthwaite had left ajar, so he didn't
catch Copperthwaite's *riposte* which was something about some
bad pennies being there all the time.

Later, when Anthony emerged at breakfast time, they seemed
to be billing and cooing.

Soon afterwards, when Copperthwaite was in his room, presumably unpacking his impressive suit-cases, Anthony said to
Olive,

'Copperthwaite has come back.'

'So I see, Mr. Easterfield,' she answered drily, and giving him
a poke, or, as some would say, a back-lash, with the carpet-
sweeper. 'So I see,' she repeated, 'and how long for?'

'Oh, I don't know,' said Anthony carelessly. 'I've no idea
what his plans are, or if he has any. You may know better than I
do.'

'I have nothing against Mr. Copperthwaite,' said Olive, drawing herself up and reclining, so far as one can recline, on the pole
of a carpet-sweeper.

'I've nothing against him,' she repeated, 'but this I know, he'll
go *when* it's his interest to go, and *where*,' she added dwelling on
the words, 'it's his interest to go.'

'Then why,' said Anthony, taking her up, 'did he leave this
much better job with the millionaire across the Square, and come
back here, where he doesn't get half as much money or half as
much time off?'

This will be a facer for her, he thought. But it wasn't.

'I wouldn't know,' she said, starting off again with the carpet-
sweeper, 'I wouldn't know what goes on in a man's mind. It
might be that this American—and not only Americans either,'
she added, giving Anthony a straight look, 'was one of those who
—well, I needn't explain. Mind you, I'm not saying anything

against Copperthwaite, but he may have felt the game wasn't worth the candle.'

'The candle?'

'You know what I mean, sir.'

'I don't,' said Anthony, although a faint flicker of enlightenment played across his mind—'but if he didn't do whatever . . . whatever they wanted him to do—isn't that a good mark for him?'

'I'm not saying it is or it isn't,' said Olive darkly. 'With those sort of people you never know. Keep away from them, I say.'

'But that's just what he has done,' said Anthony, rashly.

'Time will show,' said Oliver, who was apt to repeat her more gnomic utterances. 'Time will show.'

Anthony's curiosity, never very keen, was whetted by Olive's insinuations, and the temptation increased to ask Copperthwaite why he had left a job so much better than the one he had come back to. 'Better not,' he told himself, falling into Olive's habit of repeating herself, 'better not. All in good time, all in good time.'

The thunderous sounds of Copperthwaite's unpacking suddenly ceased, and he himself appeared at the door of Anthony's sitting-room. At least it must be he, this radiant figure dressed in the smartest chauffeur's uniform, peaked cap in hand.

'Would you be wanting me to drive you anywhere, sir?' (Sir, now, not Mr. Easterfield, as of yore.)

'Well, no, Copperthwaite,' Anthony said, rising from his chair to greet this splendid apparition, 'I've nowhere to go, and I'm not sure if the car' (he hardly liked to mention this ignoble vehicle) 'will be—well, will be in going order. You see, it hasn't been used . . .' He stopped, feeling that tactlessness must go no further.

'I see, sir,' said Copperthwaite, as if envisaging a great number of things. 'Leave it to me. But first I will put on my working clothes.' He sketched a salute to go.

'There is lunch,' said Anthony humbly.

'Oh yes, sir, I've arranged for that, and Olive has been quite helpful.'

He disappeared, and Anthony began to write some letters. What a relief to have Copperthwaite back! But when he thought

of that magnificent uniform, and its probable cost, he began to
feel uneasy. Ought not Copperthwaite, or he, Anthony, to return
it to Copperthwaite's late employers? No doubt the Americans
could well afford it; but the cynical saying 'Soak the rich,' began
to reverberate unpleasantly in his mental ear.

Should he say something to Copperthwaite? Should he suggest
that the uniform ought to be returned? When Copperthwaite was
in his employ, he had expressly wished not to wear a uniform; he
inferred it would be a badge of servitude, and in any case too
posh, too ostentatious for Anthony's humdrum purposes.
Anthony himself could imagine his friends saying, if they came
to the door to see him off, as they sometimes did, and saw his
second-hand, second-rate car waiting at the kerb, with a uniformed chauffeur—uniformed, and how!—'We are *impressed*,
Anthony, we really *are* impressed!'

No sound in the flat, but Anthony was restless, he went out and
took a turn round the square (if a square can be circled). His footsteps came slow, clogged by his thoughts. Shall I turn back? he
asked himself, seeking for some sort of compromise between himself and the Moral Law. Shall I go up to Ramoth Gilead, or shall
I forbear? Shall I tell Copperthwaite to return his ill-gotten gains
to the Americans, or shall I leave it?

At the opposite side of the Square stood the Roland-Rex (by
now he knew its contours only too well), drawn up outside the
owner's door. Sitting at the wheel, indeed asleep at the wheel,
was a chauffeur, immaculate in a uniform similar to Copperthwaite's. He looked like part of the car's furniture, indeed like
part of the car; he was the same colour, his figure might have
been an extension, as a reproduction of its lines; its immobility a
parallel of its own. Function for function, what difference was
there between them?

Anthony completed the circuit.

No car outside his own flat; but he pressed the button; the
garage-door swung open, revealing a set of loose boxes, so to
speak, in which some of the tenants kept their cars. He remembered the number of his: 5A.

At first he saw nothing except his car, then, sticking out from under its bonnet, a pair of feet and leggings.

'Copperthwaite!' he called, hardly expecting an answer.

But after much wriggling, Copperthwaite came into view, so dirty in his overalls, so changed from his glorious appearance of an hour ago, that the transformation was hardly credible.

He struggled to his feet.

'Yes, sir?'

'I just wondered,' said Anthony, 'how you were getting on?'

'Very well, sir,' said Copperthwaite, composing his face to disguise the slight irritation he felt at being disturbed at his work; 'Very well, sir. But I'm afraid the car needs a good deal of attention. It's been neglected, sir.'

Anthony said nothing.

'Yes, sir, it's been neglected, and of course a car doesn't like being neglected.'

Anthony couldn't resist saying,

'Like human beings, I suppose.'

'Yes, like human beings,' said Copperthwaite, mopping his brow with a sweaty handkerchief, and without taking, or appearing to take, Anthony's point. 'But human beings can fend for themselves.'

He gave the car an over-all look, in which compassion, interest, and adoration—yes, adoration—were blended.

The sudden impulse that makes one ask a question that one would never, in ordinary circumstances and after due consideration, ask, made Anthony say,

'Why did you leave that excellent job with the American gentleman on the other side of the Square? I thought—in fact you told me yourself—it was your ambition to look after a Roland-Rex.'

'So it was, sir,' said Copperthwaite promptly, his eyes switching to Anthony's battered car. 'And shall I tell you why—why I didn't go on there. I mean, because the money was good and the boss gave me all I wanted, including the uniform, which I didn't want. It was because—'

'Because of what?'

'The Roland-Rex was a perfect car, no complaints.'

'Then why?'

Copperthwaite gave Anthony a look that pitied such lack of understanding.

'Because there was nothing I could do for it. Nothing ever went wrong with it, it didn't need me, I couldn't—I couldn't mix myself with it—it was a stranger, if you know what I mean. I sat there like a stuffed dummy—the car could have looked after itself, and almost driven itself, without me—'

He stopped, and gave another look at Anthony's shabby old roadster.

'Your car isn't a Roland-Rex, sir, but as long as you are in it you will be driving with me as well as in it.'

Anthony found this remark obscure.

'Well, of course I shall be driving with you, because I can't drive myself, but what do you mean by, I shall be driving with you, as well as with it?'

'Because I *am* the car, sir.'

*

Anthony tried to fathom this out.

'Does the car mean all that to you?' he asked incredulously.

'It does, sir. It means a great deal to me, as you do, though not in the same way—begging your pardon, sir.'

Anthony heard the church bells ringing.

'Good gracious, it's Sunday!' he exclaimed. 'I'm all out in my dates—I wasn't expecting you till Monday.'

'Yes, but one day doesn't make much difference, does it?'

'Of course not.' Anthony wondered where Copperthwaite had spent Saturday night. 'But when I was walking round the Square I noticed that your . . . your late employer had another chauffeur.'

Copperthwaite shrugged his shoulders.

'Oh yes, Mr. Duke doesn't let the grass grow under his feet, and there are plenty of blokes who will give up their weekends if they see a good job in prospect, and a uniform too.'

The bells sounded louder. Eleven o'clock could not be far away.

'Well, I must be off,' said Anthony to Copperthwaite's retreating form, which was edging itself, feet first this time, as if some octopus power, stronger than himself, was sucking him into the tentacles of the car's dark underneath.

Rapture began to glow on Copperthwaite's upturned face.

'If you are going to church, sir,' he said, wriggling from shoulder to shoulder, 'say a prayer for me.'

'Yes, of course,' said Anthony, 'but what would it be?'

'Oh, I don't know, sir, you know more about prayers than I do, just a little prayer for me, and a big prayer for the car.'

'But isn't it past praying for?'

'No, sir, not as long as I'm here,' and with that Copperthwaite's tired, dirty, but jubilant face disappeared under the bonnet.

An answer to prayer, perhaps?

PARADISE PADDOCK

MARCUS FOSTER acquired his house, Paradise Paddock, with the maximum of discouragement from his friends. 'We looked at ninety-eight,' one of them said. 'We spent the best part of a year house-hunting, and every single one of them had something hopelessly against it. Either it faced the wrong way, or it had a cellar full of water which would have to be pumped out, or it had no water at all, no electricity and no gas, or it was so far from anywhere that such important things as food could never be delivered, and staff, supposing one could find them, would never consent to stay, and anyhow there were no suitable quarters for them to stay in, and—well, at last, when we were quite desperate, we found Wrightswell, which was so much too big that we had to pull half of it down.'

Marcus was utterly at a loss, for he felt that where his practical or comparatively practical friends, the Larkins, had failed, he was most unlikely to succeed. When he surveyed the length and breadth of England, sometimes with a map, sometimes relying on his imagination, he didn't know which way to turn.

But turn he must, for the people who had let him their house, for the period of the war, now wanted it back.

Where could he go? He was a bachelor and an orphan, aged fifty, by no means rich but not too badly off. The thought of all England lying before him, studded with houses, each of which had some vital drawback, appalled him. And what of Henry and Muriel, the couple who had served him well for so many years, in spite of Muriel's chronic melancholia and Henry's occasional outbursts of temper, where would *they* go?

Marcus was not without friends, and he decided, with an unconscious foresight, that he had better try to find a house that was near to some of them. In the town of Baswick, in the west country, he had several good friends. Baswick must be his first househunting ground.

How to start about it? Marcus found the name of a house-agent in Baswick, and applied to him.

Marcus's quest had at the same time, vis-à-vis the vast area of England, a limitation which might be a hindrance but also might be a help. He wanted a house by the river, where he could row his boat. Boating was his favourite pastime—boating of a relaxed, unskilful, unprofessional kind, just plodding along a river, in a skiff with a sliding seat, thoughtless, mindless. But something from the movement and from the rustle, heard or unheard, of Nature around him, gave him a peace of mind which he couldn't give himself.

Baswick was on a river.

The house-agent, a red-faced beefy-looking man, said, 'I think we've got just the place for you. It's called Paradise Paddock. It was occupied by the Army, and perhaps still is, but we'll go and see.'

Marcus, certain that the expedition would be a wash-out, jumped into the car, and in a quarter of an hour they were there.

It was a mill-house, the river dammed up on one side and flowing freely, but not too freely, on the other. So much Marcus took in, before, crossing a little bridge, they stood in front of a paint-blistered front-door, and the agent rang the bell.

A lady answered it, dressed in the casual clothes of an artist, as in fact she turned out to be.

'Yes?' she said.

The agent advanced a step or two.

'I understand this house is for sale,' he said.

'Well, I'm the owner of it,' she replied, 'and I can assure you it isn't.'

The agent was by no means taken aback.

'I'm sorry, Madam,' he said, 'I must have been mistaken.'

'Not to worry,' said the lady. 'Siince you've come out here, perhaps you would like to see over the house.'

It had been built at different times, and on different levels; not a room that had not a step up to it, or a step down. Not only that, they seldom faced each other squarely, they eyed each other widdershins. But Marcus liked them all.

He told the owner so. 'I'm so sorry you don't want to part with the house,' he said, when the tour was over, 'but I quite understand.'

'I didn't say I didn't want to part with it,' the woman answered, 'I only said I was the owner of it—I and my husband—and that it was not for sale. But we might change our minds, given a suitable inducement.'

'Well, perhaps you will let me know,' said Marcus, with a caution that was usual with him, for he hated decisions, and could only make them on the spur of the moment, or not at all.

'I can let you know now,' the woman said. 'We *are* prepared to sell it, if you will name a sum.'

Marcus glanced at the agent, whose porphyry-coloured face became for a moment mask-like, before he said, 'I think £5,000 would be a fair price.'

'Oh, surely,' the woman protested.

'The house isn't everyone's choice, as perhaps you know,' said the agent, giving her a look. 'I don't say it's damp, but it well may be, since there is water all round it. I doubt if you would get a higher offer.'

'I must ask my husband,' she said, showing them the door.

It hadn't occurred to the innocent Marcus that she was meaning to sell it all the time.

When he took possession, he brought with him the furniture and *objets d'art* that he had been collecting during the war years. At first they made the house, or some of it, look habitable. Later, when he had been toying with them and moving them this way and that, it looked less so. One thing that he couldn't find a suitable place for was a turquoise-coloured beetle—obviously meant to be Egyptian for it had a cartouche on its back, but too large, he thought, to be a real scarab. He had bought it at an antique shop for a few shillings.

A friend, who had travelled much in the Near East, took a different view.

'One never knows,' he said. 'I don't like the look of it and I should get rid of it, if I were you.'

Marcus, who was superficially superstitious, and hated to see a single magpie, or the new moon through glass, or to spill the salt, or break a looking-glass (which, happily, he had never done) was fundamentally anti-superstitious, and thought one shouldn't give way to it. . . .

'How have things been going here?' his friend asked.

'Oh, quite all right,' said Marcus, with an assurance that his expression belied. 'One or two people have troubles. A friend of mine fell downstairs and broke a bone in her hand, and the gardener fell down some steps which were rather greasy—it rains so much here—and had to have some stitches put into his elbow. But these things happen in the best-regulated establishments.'

'But *you* have suffered no inconvenience?' asked his friend, surveying the curious little object, with its rudimentary antennae, which looked as if they might wave.

'None,' said Marcus.

'All the same,' said his friend, 'I should get rid of the creature, if I were you. It isn't a creature, of course, but it looks rather like one.'

Months passed that were not uneventful, and his friend again came to stay.

'Well, how goes it?' he asked.

'What do you mean?'

'Well, domestically and otherwise.'

'Oh,' said Marcus, 'nothing much. My cook fell into the river, one night, looking for her cat. She dotes on it. The cat I hardly need say, was quite safe in some outhouse, and would never have dreamed of plunging into the river, especially in this cold weather. Happily, Mrs. Landslide's husband was at hand, and he hauled her out, wet through, but none the worse for her ducking. There was something else,' he added, unwillingly, 'but it happened only a fortnight ago, and I don't much want to talk about it.'

'Tell me, all the same.'

'Well—but not well—the gardener's young daughter, Christine, was riding her bicycle on the main road, coming away from school, and a lorry hit her, and well—she died. Not very nice, was it?' said Marcus, with a tremor in his voice. 'They haven't got over it, of course, and I don't suppose they ever will. They don't blame me, I'm glad to say; it was no fault of mine, though I had given the bicycle to Christine as a birthday present.'

His friend considered this.

'Have you still got that scarab?'

'Yes.'

'Well, if I were you I should get rid of it.'

'But how? It wouldn't be enough to sell it, or give it to somebody I disliked. I don't know much about black magic, but I am sure it involves some kind of ritual.'

'You're right,' said his friend, 'it does, but there are ways and means.'

'Such as?'

'Some method that combines secrecy with publicity. For instance, if you were in a railway carriage—only it must be *crowded*—'

'Yes?'

'And you threw the scarab out of the window without anyone seeing—without anyone seeing—' he repeated—'then you might break its spell. I know it sounds quite silly and there are other ways. You didn't steal it, did you?'

'No, I bought it over the counter, as I told you,' said Marcus huffily.

'What a pity. But if you could make someone *else* steal it— stealing is very important in these matters—that might do as well. Where do you keep it?'

'Locked up in a drawer. To tell you the truth, I almost never look at it. I'd rather not.'

'Well, take it out of the drawer, and put it in some prominent place—on the chimney-piece, perhaps—and see what happens.'

Marcus pondered the alternatives. He was even more loath to touch the object than he was to look at it; and what made matters worse, he despised himself for entertaining such ridiculous fancies. However, a seed sown in the subconscious mind is hard to eradicate. Events seemed to have confirmed his friend's warnings. He unlocked the drawer and, hunching his shoulders with distaste, took the 'creature' out. Its embryo whiskers, its wings, if wings they were, folded sleekly and closely on its back, disgusted him; its sinister expression alarmed him; and he went so far as to get a pair of tongs to convey it to the chimney-piece in his study.

No one will want to steal it, he told himself; I only wish they would.

Mrs Crumble, his daily help, had been several months in his employ. She cleaned and dusted and, if, as rarely happened, she broke something, she nearly always told him—rather as if it were his fault. 'You leave so many things lying about,' she complained, 'it's a wonder they don't all get broken.'

'Never mind about breaking them,' he said, 'so long as you keep the pieces. Then we can patch them together, if they're worth it.'

This she always did, but one morning he noticed a gap on the chimney-piece (for his eyes were trained towards the scarab) and a few minutes later Mrs Crumble came in with a long face.

'I'm afraid I've broken that insect, sir,' she said. 'I was only flicking it with the duster, and it fell off the ledge and broke.'

'Never mind,' said Marcus, hardly concealing his relief, and added automatically, 'Did you keep the pieces?'

'No, sir, I didn't. It was that broken that no one could have mended it, so I threw the pieces out. I hope it wasn't valuable?'

'Not at all,' said Marcus.

He was just rearranging the objects on the chimney-piece when Henry, his factotum, came in.

'I don't want to tell any tales, sir,' he said, 'but I happened to see Mrs Crumble slip that big beetle into her bag. I only say so because I don't want you to suspect that I or my wife took it. We would never do such a thing, but I thought it was only fair to us to let you know.'

'Quite right, Henry,' said Marcus.

Three days later Mrs. Crumble's daughter, a child of twelve, came in and said importantly, 'Mum isn't coming today. She's been took bad. The doctor thinks it's appendicitis.'

It turned out to be something worse than that, and within a few days Mrs. Crumble was dead.

Marcus was very much upset, and his conscience smote him, for hadn't he deliberately exposed the scarab as a bait for somebody's cupidity? Yet he couldn't help being relieved that the 'insect', the 'beetle', the 'creature', had been safely disposed of, and out of the house. Imagine, therefore, his consternation when, a few days after the funeral, the doorbell rang, with a particularly piercing buzz, and when he opened the door, there was Mrs. Crumble's daughter standing on the threshold. She was carrying, linked to her finger, a small parcel wrapped in brown paper.

'Oh, Mr. Foster,' she said, and stopped. Her eyes became moist, and tears fell from them. 'Mum told me, when she knew she had to go, to give you this. It's that beetle creature you had on your mantelpiece, she said. She said she took a fancy to it, and told you that she had broken it, but it wasn't true, and she did not want to die with a lie on her lips. Almost the last thing she did, before she was taken from us, was to wrap it up. So here it is,' said the girl, holding out the parcel for Marcus to take.

For once Marcus was able to make up his mind quickly. Never, never would he accept, above all from a dead woman's hand, a gift which had given his subconscious mind, however misguided it might be, so much anxiety.

'It was too kind of her to have thought of it,' he said, handing the parcel back, 'and too kind of you to have brought it to me. But please, *please*, keep it. It may be worth something, my dear child, I don't know; but if it is, or if it isn't, I shall be more than thankful for you to have it, in memory of your dear mother's kindness to me.'

The daughter sniffed a little, and reached for the parcel.

'It's quite pretty,' she said, doubtfully, 'but since you would like us to keep it—'

'I *should* like you to keep it,' said Marcus firmly, 'and I hope it will bring you good luck.'

Marcus again asked his superstitious friend to stay with him for a weekend. To Marcus's surprise, for his friend was punctilious in such matters, many days passed before he received an answer. The friend excused himself; he was in Rome, but would be back in a few days. 'I met several friends of yours,' he said, 'and we talked about you.' He didn't say he hoped that Marcus would renew the invitation, as he well might have, for they were old friends, but Marcus did at once renew it. At one time he had spent several winters in Rome, and apart from wanting to see his friend, he wanted to gossip about his Roman friends. So he suggested another weekend, in fact two other weekends.

'You needn't worry about the scarab,' he added, 'I have disposed of it, I'll tell you how, and the house is now exorcised and purified.'

His friend replied that he was delighted to hear this, but he could only stay over one night, as he had to be back in London on Sunday evening.

Marcus was slightly hurt by this, but reminded himself of the danger of getting touchy as one grew older.

They talked of many things, of their Roman acquaintances, who seemed to have grown more vivid to Marcus with the passing years when, inevitably, of the 'occurrences' at Paradise Paddock.

'What have you done with that scarab?' his friend asked.

'Oh,' said Marcus negligently, 'my daily help stole it.'

'What happened then?'

'Oh, then she died. It was very, very sad. But she needn't have stolen it, need she? I didn't ask her to.' He still felt guilty.

'I think you have been lucky,' said his friend, looking round him and sniffing the air. 'I think—I *think* so, Marcus.'

The open door of the study gaped, at an acute angle, on the open door of the dining-room.

'It's strange how right you have been,' said Marcus. 'I must confess, I didn't really believe you about the scarab, but then I was brought up in a sceptical atmosphere. My father—' he paused—'well, he was a rationalist. You half convinced me—but only half. Calamities happen in every house—this isn't the only one. You know that local people call it The House of Death?'

'I didn't know.'

'Well, they do and the reason may be that for two hundred years it has been called Paradise Paddock—the association between Death and Paradise is rather encouraging and beautiful, I think. Out of one, into the other.'

His friend fixed his eye on the open doorway.

'Should we go for a little walk, do you think? I sleep badly, as you know, and they say, "After dinner, walk a mile".'

'A mile is rather a long way,' said Marcus, 'but let us take a turn, by all means. Only it will have to be mostly on the pavement—the road, with all this traffic, is really dangerous.'

'I *would* like a breath of fresh air,' his friend said.

They started off, following the pavement. Under the street lamps the traffic roared beside them.

'Shall we go back now?' Marcus asked.

His friend turned his head in the direction in which Paradise Paddock presumably lay.

A little onwards lend thy guiding hand
To these dark steps—a little further on,
he quoted, obviously unwilling to return.

They proceeded, and it was then that Marcus's friend, catching his foot on the kerb, fell headlong. To Marcus's consternation he didn't pick himself up, but lay on his back, one leg tucked under him, the other stretched out at an unnatural angle.

Marcus tried to help him to his feet, but he resisted.

Writhing a little, he turned his screwed face towards the street-lamp overhead, which invested it with a yellowish pallor and gasped, between broken breaths, 'Thank you for only breaking my leg—you might have killed me. Did no one ever tell you you had the Evil Eye?'

ROMAN CHARITY

IN some day and age which I won't try to identify—it might be now—Rudolph Campion was sent to prison. Campion wasn't his real name; it was a name he had assumed partly because some of his forbears were English, which was then, and still sometimes is, a recommendation, something to put on a passport, or what served him as a passport, for he had more than one. Rudolph Campion, Englishman. He himself could hardly remember what his real name was. It certainly wasn't English; but then, as now, it was a disadvantage to be stateless, especially for someone who travelled about the world as much as Rudolph Campion did.

Living such a nomadic life, it was surprising that Rudolph was married, and not so much that he was married, as that he still had married ties. His wife had left him, bored with his itinerate life, in one of the countries that he from time to time frequented; she wanted to settle down, she said, and not always be a camp-follower, often living under canvas, whatever the weather. So at some point in his wanderings, not too far from a capital city where such civilization as recent wars had left, still remained, she told him she had had enough, and would seek her fortune in this city; she did not say how.

In her late thirties, she was almost as good-looking as he was; in fact if it hadn't been for his good looks—bearded, moustachioed, with thinning hair, unkempt and shaggy—a man of today he might have been—she wouldn't have stuck to him as long as she did. But there were other men with equal physical attractions, who liked a settled life, and a home, and she didn't despair of finding one.

It took her some time to come to this decision, for had they not been married twenty years? and she, like many women in this and other ways more far-sighted than men, valued a stable personal relationship. This she had enjoyed with Rudolph (Rudy to her, though never rude). He might have strayed; he probably had; but she was not upset by the suspicion of his possible infidelities, when he was out of sight (as he so often was) but not out of mind. He always came back to her, and was as loving as he was loved; and though she didn't really know, and didn't much want to know, what his actual business was, although she did know that an element of danger attended it, when they pitched their moving tent a day's march nearer a destination in this country or in that, his friends, for he had friends or accomplices in many countries, knew that she came first with him. The news of their relationship seemed to precede them: she never had to explain who she was; she was accepted, in whatever society, as belonging to him and he to her; a good-looking and above all, an inseparable couple. The personal vanity, the sense of being esteemed for their own sake, which many people and most women have, was amply satisfied for Trudi by her Rudy—a joke which his friends, who were seldom hers, often made. Never could she remember a time when, however little she had to do with the business in hand, Rudi had pressed her to make herself agreeable to some hard-faced little man, on whose favour, or favours, success depended. She might have yielded, for Rudi left her much alone, and as the Italian proverb says, 'One gets tired of home-made bread.'

No, in their twenty years together he had never, so to speak, pushed her into a corner, never made her feel that she was just an adjunct, a useful business-asset, but otherwise rather a drag. Perhaps he hardly could have, for she couldn't enter a room without making her beauty felt.

All this she realized; but as the rain dripped through the canvas of the tent—they didn't always live in a tent, but between times they had to when they were on the run—she said to her daughter who shared two-thirds of the tent with her, the other third being curtained off for sleeping-quarters, and other masculine requirements. Rudy didn't seem to mind the dripping rain.

'Angela, I think I shall have to make a change. I'm very proud of your father, but this sort of life doesn't suit me. It may be all right for a man, but I'm getting too old for it. And now that you're engaged to be married—'

'I was married yesterday, Mother, but you were so busy with one thing and another, I didn't like to tell you.'

The mother and daughter turned to each other on their dampening beds.

'You didn't like to tell me?'

'No, I thought it was kinder not to.'

'Speak lower, he might hear you,' Angela began to whisper.

'Oh no, he sleeps like a log. But I know I'm a responsibility to you in the odd life he makes you lead, so when Jacko asked me to marry him—'

'Jacko?'

'Yes, you've seen him several times. Well, I said yes.'

'Jacko?'

'Yes, he's got a job as a courier, and we like each other. I mightn't have done it, but I knew it was a strain for you, living with Father, in these conditions, and with me in tow. I didn't know that you were going to take the step of leaving him—but I would have married Jacko even if I had known you had—.'

'Jacko?'

'Yes, he's a nice fellow, a reliable sort.'

'You're sure?'

'Oh yes, quite sure. He's not a substitute for Father, whom I've always loved, just as you have, and shall always love. But I can't *do* anything for him, any more than you can. He's a lone wolf, and picks up his living wherever he can find it. I don't think we need feel sorry for him—he'll always fall on his feet. But I shall always keep in touch with him, as no doubt you will, and if ever he gets into a jam—'

'I shall hear what he says, I shall hear what he says,' said her mother. 'At any rate he will have you to fall back on.'

'Yes, always.'

'Jacko or no Jacko?'

'Yes, Father will always mean more to me than anyone. And to you, Mother?'

'I'm not quite so sure. Twenty years is a long time. I'll tell him tomorrow.'

They listened to the dropping of the rain, a soothing sound, before they too dropped off.

So next day Rudy learned that in a very short time he was to be wife-less and daughter-less.

In those days, as in these, political prisoners were not always well-treated and if they fell into the wrong hands—and there were a good many wrong hands to fall into, no matter whom they might be working for—their lot was not likely to be a happy one. It was a risk of Rudy's trade—his international trade—and he was prepared to accept it, just as any man who engages in one of the many sports and occupations which involve risk to life and limb, is prepared to accept it. Indeed, it was no doubt the risk attached to his present job, whatever it was, that made him choose it; he wouldn't have been happy in a humdrum occupation where no danger lurked. No thrill, no wondering if he would just turn the corner, no spice of life.

And so far it had worked quite well. There had been anxious moments when he was glad to have his car outside; moments when his command of languages (he had been brought up to know three) suddenly failed him; moments when some suspicious looking stranger followed him to the door, and asked for his address. He would give an address, an imaginary address, and within an hour or two he and Trudi would be far away, pitching their tent; and Angela would be with them. The tent was in the boot of the car, and they had brought pitching it to a fine art; in half an hour or so it would be ready and soon afterwards a delicious meal would be ready, too; for Rudy was a big man and a hungry and a thirsty man; leading the life he did, with much strain on his nervous and physical constitution, he couldn't go without sustenance for long. Both his wife and his daughter enjoyed seeing him tuck into his food and swallowing down a bottle of wine. There was another bottle for them, too, if his mission had been successful. What matter if they were on the run? Being on the run brings appetite and thirst.

But now things were different, and in more ways than one. No longer was Rudy able to make his entrée into an assemblage, perhaps unfamiliar to him, and unfamiliar with him, as a family man with a beautiful wife, and a hardly less beautiful daughter, moving slowly and gracefully maturing, through her adolescence. No longer could he divert the attention of the company from him to them, while he had a quiet talk with someone he wanted to have a word with, and who might want to have a word with him. He didn't exactly take refuge behind them; but they were his cards of identity; while they were around, engaging the others in conversation, he didn't have to wonder much if people were looking at him.

Now all this was changed. The semi-social life on which so much of his success as an agent (an agent for whom? for what?) depended, had lost its context.

*

Rudy was a man of action, and action, such as it was, and wherever it was, involved a good deal of danger. This he not only accepted, he welcomed it for he was made that way; but being a professional, he didn't go in search of it; to avoid it was as much a matter of self-training and self-discipline as to confront when it came.

These two complementary qualities had helped him to get out of a number of tight places. His wife and his daughter had helped him, too, not physically, for he never wanted them to run unnecessary risks; but by their mere presence, which gave him an air of respectability and solidity which deceived a good many people.

How far he valued them for themselves, and not just as adjuncts to his appearance and personality—his image—he himself would have found it hard to say. While they were with him it was a

question he did not even ask himself: he took their presence, and
what they did for him, and what he did for them, for granted.
They were reciprocal services in a good cause. The cause of what?
Freedom perhaps, though freedom is such an elastic term; and
some of his co-adjutors wondered which side he was on. But
business is business, and as someone has said, a lie in business is
not a lie. Rudy had availed himself, cautiously of course, of this
precept.

Now he had to explain himself. It wasn't difficult to explain
that his wife was tired of travelling, which was true, and was now
living in Warsaw, which was not true. For his sake, as well as
Trudi's and Angela's, he did not want their whereabouts to be
known. He also explained, which was true, that Angela was married and expecting a baby—he did not say where, for who knew
where, or where not, a baby might be born?

This freedom from family ties gave him as a man who was still
attractive to women, a good many opportunities which he was not
slow to take; not only from the amorous angle, whatever that
might be, but from the information sometimes supplied. He
knew that information was double-edged, but he relied on getting
more than he gave.

But he was not heartless, and though not yet forty, he sometimes thought rather wistfully in the loneliness of his leaking tent,
pitched between somewhere and somewhere, or between nowhere
and nowhere, eating his viands, on which he relied so much, out
of a tin, or tins, in his solitary confinement, of the domestic
amenity and seeming security he had once enjoyed. Those softer
moments! When he came back tired and hungry from some
mission, and smelt from afar the smell of a delicious dish that was
cooking for him on the little oil stove, and heard, from nearer to,
the gentle muffled swish and a rustle, so different from a man's
direct and decisive movements—loudly proclaiming their object
instead of trying to conceal it—of the participants who were preparing his evening meal! Mouth-watering prospect! And more
than living up to its promise. While he was eating he didn't talk
much; just a word here and there escaped the otherwise inarticu-

late smacking of his lips. But afterwards, full-fed, finishing the bottle of wine or spirits, if they were in funds, for he could drink at a sitting a bottle of brandy or sligovitz, or vodka, or grappa, or calvados or whatever might be the spirituous tipple of the country; then he became expansive, and told them a little, but not (for their own sakes) too much of what he had been doing during the day—the contacts he had made, the possible development, and their probable next destination. To all this they listened eagerly, even avidly, and fondly watched his face as (unknown to him) its taut features slowly relaxed to reveal a husband and a father.

And afterwards, when the dividing curtain was drawn he could hear their lowered voices (whispers meant not to disturb him rather than to prevent him hearing what they said), after which he dropped off in a genial alcoholic haze, with a sense of protective influences round him, and replete in every sense, he slept like the proverbial log, till dawn, or until the clock in his subconscious mind (as reliable and less noisy than an alarum clock) told him it was time to get up. Even if he had possessed an alarum clock he would not have used it, for it would have disturbed the slumbers beyond the curtain (not the Iron Curtain) and sometimes he was off before day-break.

Comfort! Comfort! He might not have admitted it to himself, but it was comfort that he missed, and business, however much it may sharpen the other faculties, does not always warm the heart.

He had had many surprises in his life, his life as an international spy, but the greatest and the most unforeseen was when almost simultaneously his wife and his daughter decided to leave him. He had always been ready, as indeed he had to be, to accept facts—but he could hardly credit this one. Leave him, after twenty years of wifehood, and perhaps longer still of daughterhood? He couldn't and didn't blame them; blame didn't come into his code of behaviour, in which success and failure were his only criteria. He knew he hadn't been a good husband and father, but there were many worse; he might have treated them as camp-followers but they were willing to be so treated; he had shared his good times as well as his bad times with them, and set aside some money for them, which was no doubt one reason why they had left him. He had counted on their loyalty, not on their love; love was a thing he didn't take into account, except in the crudest way, as leading to someone or something.

All the same, in those lonely nights in the tent, when he heard no whispering of women's voices, and smelt no smell of the creature comforts they were preparing for him, he knew he was missing something. It never entered his mind that they might be missing something too.

He didn't often sleep now, as aforetime he used to, in the comfort of a luxury hotel; but sometimes he did, and it was there that the unexpected happened. In the middle of dinner, with a bottle of wine half empty on the table, two men touched him on the shoulder and before he had time to pay his bill, or anyone had time to pay it for him, he was marched away and bundled into a waiting car, not his car, which was outside in the car-park. 'Can't I get my things?' he asked in the language of the country. 'No, we've got all your things that matter,' was the reply, and no more was said until he found himself, handcuffed, in a small cell, seven feet by five with a grated window at the top, admitting the air, and a grated window in the door, admitting a dim light from the passage. An unshaded bulb hanging from the ceiling showed him a straw mattress in the corner, and one or two pieces of furniture which might have been made out of the same substance as the cell.

Here they left him; but presently a warder came in with a small bundle of clothes which he recognized as his. 'This is all you'll want,' he said, 'we've got the rest. I'll show you where the place is,' and unlocking the door he indicated where Rudy could relieve himself. 'But you'll have to knock on the door—there's always me or one of us in the passage. Lights out at ten o'clock. Breakfast at six. These handcuffs are a bit tight, I'll give you some second-grade ones, and you can stretch your arms a bit. No fooling about, mind. Good-night.'

The new handcuffs did indeed give Rudy more freedom of movement. Instead of being clamped together, with only an interval of a few inches between, hardly enough, not enough, to enable him to satisfy the most rudimentary needs of Nature, his hands now stretched to his hips; he could feel parts of his body that before had been beyond their scope; he could have picked things up from the dirty stone floor, had there been anything worth picking up. He could even embrace himself, or part of himself, had he felt so inclined. This freedom! But compared with the earlier restriction it seemed like liberty. Now he could sleep again; he had always been a good sleeper, but with his hands tied so tight in front of or (according to the gaoler's whim) behind him, he had been unable to sleep, and his breakfast of bread and water, or whatever insubstantial substance took its place, found him more tired than he had been at ten o'clock lights out.

But now, folding and unfolding his arms so as to give him as little discomfort, not to say pain, as might be, he awoke, not refreshed, but with the blessed sense of having slept.

Gradually he adjusted himself, as best he could, to his new life. Small reliefs, that in the old days he would have taken for granted or not noticed—the cleansing of his cell from certain noxious insects—seemed like a gift from Heaven. And what a blessing it was to go out into the light of common day and join the other prisoners in their half-hours exercise inside the high-walled courtyard. Here they were allowed to speak to each other, those who had the necessary gift of speech, for they were of many nations and languages. Some had known each other recently, some from long ago; but the majority, of whom Rudy was one, were too low-spirited to want to talk much. What was there to talk about, between those flat, encircling walls, outside which life went on, with its incentives and excitements, whereas inside all was static and uneventful, without hope, promise, or future? Only death; and for death he sometimes longed. He couldn't understand why he hadn't been executed before; 'they' had plenty against him, a whole dossier, and from time to time they made him stand up in his cell while they questioned him. Sometimes he was too weak to stand up, and asked permission to sit down on his straw bed. He answered, or parried the questions as well as he could, and as well as his tired mind would let him. He had to keep a constant watch on his tongue, for he didn't want to involve other people more than he could help—it was an occupational obligation to keep his mouth, as far as might be, shut.

He wasn't subjected to any physical or bodily torture, in these interrogations, except a very hard strong light from an electrical instrument they brought with them, shining on his eyes. It dazzled and distressed him, and drove almost every thought from his head; to keep his head, or what remained of it, was his chief concern.

They are trying to wear me down, he thought, they are trying to wear me down, and perhaps one day they will, and perhaps I shall tell them everything—what is true as well as untrue—for he knew only too well, that for some psychological reason, physical or even emotional pressure will induce a man to tell the truth, instead of the lies to which spies are accustomed and which they have already carefully prepared.

They are waiting for me to break down, he thought, they are waiting for me to break down, and he who had always been proud of his strength, felt this as an almost personal affront to his image of himself.

Meanwhile his fears for his health were being too well justified. Needless to say, there was no looking glass in his cell—why should a prisoner want to look at himself? much better not. They had taken away his razor, as no doubt they do, and always have done, in many prisons, and for obvious reasons: but they had left him his little pocket mirror, in which, in better days, he used to study his face to see if it looked like what he wanted it to look like at the moment.

And now, what a picture did it present! He had usually been clean-shaven; he had sometimes, when the occasion seemed to demand it, been bearded; but beards need a good deal of attention and in the absence of scissors, his face, as he saw it reflected, was almost unrecognisable, and also shaming, for he had always been proud of his looks which had taken him a long way on his uneven road to temporary prosperity.

And now another thing, another physical thing, connected with the conditions in which he lived. The chain of his handcuffs had been considerably lengthened, so that he could now scratch himself (an almost necessary activity) in places where before he could not; but owing to his hands and wrists being of extra size, they chafed him, bringing to those parts sores and inflammation which took away what little physical comfort he had left. His gaoler, who was by no means unsympathetic, for a gaoler, reported this to the prison doctor, and the doctor, seeing Rudy's swollen and suppurating hands, recommended handcuffs at least an inch wider, to help circulation and enable the blood to flow. This was a great relief to Rudy, whose robust constitution responded to any mitigation allowed it, and by degrees, the swelling died down, leaving behind them hollows where the flesh and muscles used to be.

Being technically stateless, though he had (or had had, before his belongings were confiscated), more than one passport he could not appeal to any country for aid, and even if he could have, the country he appealed to would certainly not have recognized him. Now that spying was an almost organized occupation, he had hoped that he might be exchanged for some opposite number (he could think of several); but it hadn't happened—for how could he get in touch with some country to whom he had been of service? It didn't seem likely to happen. In fact he had no one in authority to appeal to; and meanwhile he grew thinner, and less and less, physically and mentally, his old self.

For it was his misfortune that the country which had caught up with him and detected him was a poor country, and overrun by refugees; they had no food to spare for themselves or for the refugees, political sympathisers, who swarmed over them; and those who came last on the list, for physical sustenance, were political prisoners, of whom, for one reason and another, they had a surfeit.

Rudy's diet was hardly enough to keep body and soul together;

looking at himself, when he was allowed to have a bath, as sometimes the prisoners were, he hardly recognized the fine figure of a
man he used to know.

*

Occasionally, but only occasionally, and under the strictest supervision, the prisoners were allowed to receive visitors. Such
visitors, of course, had to be carefully 'screened', and more often
than not, they were turned away at the gateway of the prison. So
what was Rudy's surprise, when his gaoler told him, almost as if
it was a command not a concession, that a lady wanted to see him.
'She says she is your daughter. I don't know if you know about
her. But sometimes we let in relations.'

'Just a moment, please,' said Rudy, who was lying on his bed,
half naked, owing to the intense heat. 'Just a moment.' He tried
to collect his thoughts, if any, but the sound of running water in
the lavatory at the end of the passage gave him, as it gives many
men, an uncontrollable desire to pee. 'Take me down there, will
you?' he said, waving towards the sound, for without the gaoler's
permission, and presence, he couldn't relieve the needs of Nature.

'All right, but hurry up,' the gaoler said, 'Ten minutes is the
most you'll be allowed.'

'I shan't need ten minutes here,' answered Rudy, on the
threshold of the *pissoir*.

Natural needs, as so often they do, brought him to a sense of
his general situation. Who was it who wanted to see him? For
weeks, months, it seemed, he had been cut off from contact with
the outside world. He had given up hope of ever seeing it again.
He hardly even wanted to see it, so inured had he become not
only to the privations but to the utter lack of personal incentive,
the desire to make himself known and felt, which is the almost
inevitable consequence of even a short spell in prison.

'Hurry up,' repeated the warder, just behind him. 'You've only
got ten minutes.'

Rudy followed him back, and in a few moments the door of his
cell re-opened.

'Father!' she exclaimed, but she recognized him before he recognized her, this glorious young creature, dressed in what he imagined was the height of fashion, pearls, bracelets, even a little tippet of fur in case the broiling evening should turn cold.

They embraced and embraced, her beautifully attired body to his half-naked one. But it was the body of her father.

When her tears began to dry she said,

'But you're so *thin*!'

'They don't give us much to eat here,' he said, as casually as he could.

His daughter had of course seen him in 'his prime', how many months ago? when the shield of partition between his sleeping-quarters and theirs, opened to reveal a half-clad figure, asking for something—probably a drink—disappearing almost as soon as it appeared—leaving behind a scent of unwashed masculinity, soon to be washed, for Rudy was particular about that and always had his white-enamelled basin, and his soap, and his washing flannel ready—for anything that might occur. Now he had none of these, he couldn't even wash, except under supervision.

This question of personal cleanliness was uppermost in his thoughts when he drew away from his daughter and said,

'You must find me very changed.' She mistook his meaning and said, 'Of course you're not changed, dear Father, except for those nasty handcuffs, and because you look so *thin*. What can we do about that?'

'Nothing,' said Rudy, 'so far as I know. This miserable country can't afford to give its subjects let alone its refugees, let alone its prisoners, a decent meal, so why should I be favoured?'

His daughter didn't answer for a moment; she knew their time together was getting short; she could see the gaoler pacing up and down the passage, with an eye on his watch for he was soon to be off duty, and a look through the grille inside to see how things were going on. Darkly his helmet gleamed.

With the sudden impulse of a woman Angela said, 'There's something I *can* do. If you agree to it, Father. Only we have to be quick.'

Smiling at him with the intensity of affection she had always felt for him, she raised her right hand to her black velvet bodice; her left hand, lovely-fingered, played around her waist in a vague semi-circle, as if awaiting a cue from the other. Her head bent forward; her smile grew more inviting as if it was the very messenger of love.

He was sitting on his straw bed, she on the hard chair opposite. He looked at her with incomprehension, alarm, almost hostility.

'What do you mean?'

The beautiful hand drew down her black velvet bodice, and exposed her breasts. 'I have a wet nurse,' she said, 'should I need one, but I have plenty of this to spare.'

For a moment Rudy could say nothing. He, who had relied so much on eating and drinking, had spent many weeks almost deprived of both. He fixed his altered face, so pale and shrunken within its covering of untutored hair, on his daughter's, beautiful in itself, still more beautified by art.

'What do you mean, Angela?'

She said nothing, but with a still warmer smile, leaned, full-bosomed, towards him.

Then he took the meaning, and wracked by thirst and hunger, took, like a child, what she offered him; nor did he desist until the shadow of the warder, passing the grille, warned him that the feast must be finished.

He wiped his mouth.

'Another time, another time?' he murmured.

'Yes,' she said, but before they had time to say more, the warder was in the cell.

'Now you must go, Madam,' he said.

*

His daughter's visit, and her gift of fresh milk, so different from the milk he was used to, so long in bottle and so often sour, completely changed Rudy's whole outlook. He was not forgotten! He was still in contact with the world outside! And with his own family! Until now he hadn't realised how much they meant to him; at the thought of them his whole being seemed to revive. He hadn't time to ask Angela how, or where, her mother was; he hadn't time to ask her how she had tracked him down; he hadn't time to ask the hundred questions he wanted to ask. He had been, quite literally, like a baby at the breast, whose one desire is to slake its thirst and its hunger and can only utter inarticulate sucking sounds meanwhile. In the process he lost all sense of shame; he didn't feel that he, a grown man, should not be finding this kind of sustenance from anyone, least of all his daughter; he didn't care that the warder, passing and re-passing his cell, could see through the small iron grille just what was happening; his physical need was so great that it quite overcame all civilized feelings. He was a starving animal, and nothing more.

When she had gone his mood began to change. The renascence which her presence, and her present, brought him didn't at once fade; the first sustained his spirit, and the second his body. It was surprising how much better he felt for both—united to the world, not only the outside world, which he could only dimly perceive through the grating in his cell, or a little more amply, over the shoulders of the surrounding walls—but to the world of the flesh which, in the days of his triumphant health, he had always taken for granted. The idea of being *ill* was too ridiculous!

But since his daughter's visit he realised how far he had gone downhill (down-ill, he thought, for he had English in his blood and was still capable of a play on words). Not only was he unattractive to look at, as his little mirror showed him, but his invincible health was failing him. Angela with the benison of her breast, had for a day or two restored it: but when, if ever, could he expect to see her again?

He knew, and had always accepted the conditions of the kind of life he led; but foresight, and experience are very different things.

If only she would come again! It wasn't only his thirsty mouth that asked this question and his whole physical system, deprived of all the dainties that used to succour it; it was the longing for *home*, not that he had ever had since he could remember a real home, but somewhere, however transient it might be, where he could *expand*, take his shoes off, throw his clothes down, asking nobody's permission, and then expect a good hot meal; and later, if he wasn't too tired, but he was never tired, the dividing curtain would come down, and Angela would take his place outside and he her place inside, as the case might be.

How far away it seemed from his present life, if life it could be called. Angela's visit had brought back a whiff of it which recalled the happy past; but as it faded, left a feeling of unbearable desolation. She would never come again, she would never come again! It would have been better if she had never come at all.

*

She did come, however. The gaoler, with a faint smirk, said, 'There's a lady to see you. The same one as last time. Shall I let her in?'

'Of course,' said Rudy, hardly believing his ears. But he had to believe his eyes.

She looked too ravishing! Among the prison visitors who could have looked like her?

When the gaoler ushered her in he warned, 'Fifteen minutes, mind, and no larking about.'

An extra five minutes was something. After their embracements, which lasted longer than before, and longer than they ever had in the days of Rudy's prosperity when the life of action had seemed so much more important than domestic felicity, her right hand, her white hand, moved as before to the black velvet of her *corsage*, the invitation in her eyes and lips was overwhelming; her left hand, just as white with its slender, curling fingers, lay as it were on guard, in case, in case—of what? Rudy did not ask himself; he stared at his daughter with greedy, staring, incredulous eyes, and eyebrows raised so high that their ridges made semicircles reaching far up his forehead.

While he was slaking his hunger and his thirst he was oblivious, as he had been before, to what was going on outside; he did not hear the warder's wary footsteps crossing and re-crossing the door of his cell, or see the helmeted head as it peered inwards.

After a while he drew away like a breast-fed child that has had its fill; and then became aware of the reality round him, his own semi-nakedness which, in spite of its emaciation, still preserved and perhaps emphasized the beauty of his body, contrasting with and yet recalling her fullness and healthiness of form, and the facial likeness between them, as she drew her velvet mantle round her.

'Aren't you rather hot in that?' he asked idly, with a father's instinctive privilege to criticize, and wiping the sweat off his chest with the weekly handkerchief the prison laundry allowed him.

'Oh no, darling, it's much colder outside than it is in here. And besides—'

'Besides?'

'Well, I have to be in the fashion. I should be wearing this even if I was on the equator.'

The time was running short. Rudy tried desperately to think of things he wanted to ask his daughter; questions he could ask without risk, and which could be answered without risk, for he didn't know whether his cell was wired for listening in.

'How is Trudi?'

'Very well, I see her quite often. She has people looking after her, I think she's all right.'

'And you, Angela?'

'Yes, I'm all right too. Jacko is a nice fellow'—and she indicated her bracelets and her necklace.

'And he doesn't mind you coming here?' asked Rudy, aware almost for the first time of the claims of personal relationships, as distinct from those of business.

'He doesn't know, and if he did, he wouldn't mind.'

'You're sure he wouldn't?'

Angela made a wide gesture with her arms, her beautiful arms, a very feminine version of her father's, which had nothing left but the bones and muscles.

'And you will be able to come and see me again?'

She smiled.

'Why not?'

The grating of the opening door, the warder's face, dark under his helmet.

'It's time, please,' he said, though the words were a command, not a request.

Angela rose and kissed her father, and then, bestowing a grateful smile on the grim-faced warder, she departed.

Where has she gone? thought Rudy. In his job it was safer not to ask people their destinations, and still safer not to reveal his own. Safer not to disclose his own locality, little as it mattered, for it wasn't a destination—if only it had been!—and perhaps he was safer here than anywhere else. He hadn't been subjected to a formal interrogation or tortured, except by the glare of the electric torch, from which his eyes still sometimes ached and smarted, it could have been much, much worse. Deep within himself, he didn't think he would escape alive. He was stateless, or rather he had too many states, too many passports, to appeal to any single one: they would all disown him, and none of those he had worked for, as he had so often reminded himself, would want to exchange him for another spy. He awaited his fate.

And yet, since Angela's second visit, his fate seemed less gloomy than before. Not less settled, not less determined; but somehow less lonely, less beyond the scope and reach and sympathy of ordinary mortals, who lived square vegetable lives, hail-brother-well-met characters, with no problems other than domestic or financial—nothing to compare with the aspect of a firing squad, or whatever agent of death awaited him.

And yet, apart from the physical stimulus, greater than the ordinarily well-fed businessman or working-man could conceive, coming from his daughter's breast, was something more emotional and more spirited—something that might have been experienced by a baby, who was not old enough to have had any other experience. A feeling of security, of not having to depend on others outside his ken, still less on himself, for his livelihood—in both senses of the word—returned to him. It didn't convince his mind; his mind still knew he was under sentence of death; but it did release, in his subconscious mind, a feeling of hope.

If Angela had twice come to see him, might she not come a third time, bringing with her the inestimable benefit of her breast and the different but equally inestimable benefit of her presence?

She did come again, quite soon, within a week; and in the joy of their reunion it didn't occur to Rudy that this was odd, considering, as he knew, that the prisoners were only allowed visitors once a fortnight.

'Don't tell Trudi where I am,' he whispered, as his daughter was letting fall her dress, silk this time, for even she had come to feel that comfort was preferable to fashion, but black still, because it suited her and showed off her white skin and her lovely hands. 'I'd rather she didn't know where I was, just tell her I'm alive.'

Angela nodded. She was now wearing her hair in a new style, piled up on the back of her head: it suited her nose which (like Cleopatra's?) was a shade too long; and the coronal of hair, into which she had introduced fragmentary gleams of shining metal, perhaps silver, balanced it.

Of this Rudy, intent upon his meal, was no more aware than a baby would have been.

Afterwards she lingered with him, talking about the outside world, which had become almost an illusion to Rudy, so distant was it from his personal experience. And then he heard her say—an interpolation in a quite different context—'I know the way out.'

He nodded in answer, for words might be overheard, and soon after, the door opened to its minimal extent, and the warder said, glancing at Angela, 'I'm afraid you must go now, Madam.'

Rudy kissed his daughter; after all that was allowed; and surrendered her to the warder. For some reason for which he couldn't rationally account, he put his ear to the grille which gave him little vision of what was going on in the passage, but did allow him to listen to their retreating footsteps.

Angela's third visit had renewed his interest in existence: he thought of himself as potentially alive, not as dead. It is always a blessing to exchange resignation for hope? Rudy couldn't tell, but he knew that hope was stirring in him. 'I know the way out,' Angela wouldn't have said that inadvertently. 'The way out' of what? There were so many predicaments to know, or not know, the way out of, with many of which Rudy was familiar; emotional situations, financial situations, all sorts of situations. Did she mean the way out of prison?

Lying on his palliasse, under his blanket, more heavy than warm (sometimes he threw it off because of the heat) he tried to make sure what Angela meant. As a rule a good sleeper, and still a good sleeper now that he had accommodated himself to his chains, he tossed and turned, and suddenly one of his hands came free from its manacles. He could hardly believe it, but so it was; his right hand was loose, it could do whatever it wanted, or he wanted it to do, scratch him, stroke him, anything. Amazing! And suddenly it came to him why, and how this had happened. Several weeks—months?—of semi-starvation had so reduced his physical frame that his hands and wrists, which used to be larger, as well as stronger, than most men's had shrivelled, had shrunk to under-handcuff size. He hadn't freed himself; his captors had freed him, to a certain very limited extent, simply by not giving him enough to eat.

Cautiously, because he still couldn't believe it, he tried with his left hand. A little wriggling, and out it came from its iron clasp. His arms were free!

He lay in or on his bed, moving them about, touching parts of himself that had long been out of touch, his feet, his legs, his chest, his chin, his head, the small of his back, all the anatomy of himself which for so many weeks, so many months, had been as unreal, as meaningless, as a map of the world—his world—long out of date.

Leaving the gyves and the chain which connected them under the diseased blanket, he got up and walked about his cell, exulting in his freedom. But only for a moment; although it was dark it wasn't safe; he could hear the gaoler's footsteps, perambulating outside; and although the gaoler must have heard many a sleepless prisoner pacing his cell, it wouldn't do to awake suspicion.

Rudy went back to bed (if the phrase is not too misleading) and after some effort, fixed on his handcuffs again. He waited for a while, to enjoy his sense of freedom; but when he realised that without his familiar bandages he wouldn't sleep (let alone the danger of being found without them in the morning) he put them on again. How blessed can confinement be, once one is used to it!

Rudy had been used to it, at any rate resigned to it, until these irruptions of his daughter's presence renewed his taste, not only for the taste of her bosom, of which, much as he relished it and felt the better for it, he was secretly ashamed, as for the free world outside these walls, where he could express himself as a man should and even order his own food!

Meanwhile he dared not take off his manacles, except in the privacy (the only privacy he had) of his bed, and didn't know what to do with his new-found freedom.

The next time Angela came she was dressed to kill. Even Rudy who like many men (and many women, for that matter) could hardly believe that a relation so close to him as a child, could be outstandingly beautiful. Trudi was a good-looking woman; Rudy as he had cause to know, was or had been, a fine figure of a man. But that between them they should have begotten this wonderful-looking creature! For almost the first time in his life Rudy had a sense of physical inferiority. Other kinds of inferiority he had often felt: social inferiority, financial inferiority, mental inferiority; but physical inferiority, no. With his clothes on, or without them, he had always been as good as, or better than, the next man.

And then to have sired this worshipful creature!

'A poor thing, but mine own.' Rudy didn't know the quotation, but he had the humility to feel, just as an equal, perhaps greater, number of people have not, that a home-made product is less to be esteemed in the eyes of the world than a shop-made product which has had the advantage of advertisement and public acclaim. Angela had neither: she was just the daughter of him and Trudi, and the idea that she had looks to attract general attention, such as a film-star might have, had never occurred to him.

Yet why had the gaoler given her and him these special privileges, for today no time-limit had been set on their intercourse?

Something moved in Rudy's mind, and when their lunch(?), tea(?), dinner (?) was over, he wiped his mouth with his weekly handkerchief, and said, and meant it, 'I am so grateful to you, darling.' He stopped, shocked and astonished at this verbal expression of emotion, which he had perhaps remembered from some film. 'What I mean is,' he amended, 'it is good of you to come and see your old dad, who isn't like what he used to be.'

He glanced at himself, as much as he could see; the famous muscles were there, especially the bunch of deltoid like a cricket-ball on his right shoulder, of which he used to be proud, and which was the more in evidence now that his flesh had receded from it. 'You've been kind to me, Angela,' he ended lamely, 'and so has Trudi, though I don't want her to know, as I told you, where I am. I don't know how you found out, for that matter.'

He didn't expect an answer, but he suddenly felt a slip of paper in his hand, and a flood of light dawned on him.

'Eat it, and when he fetches me, hit him as hard as you can.'

They looked at each other. Rudy swallowed the paper and realised what a woman, whose beauty was taken for granted by him and many others, might mean to a sex-starved prison-warder.

It explained a lot; it explained why Angela had been admitted to his cell, more often than other visitors would have been. It explained why their times together had been prolonged beyond the statutory limit. It explained—

Rudy put on his jacket to cover his nakedness, or semi-naked-ness, for he still had his trousers, and his shoes, the white gym-shoes he wore for exercise.

'Do I look all right?' he asked, buttoning up his jacket.

It was then he remembered his handcuffs. He was still wearing them, the chain between them sagged over his thighs. Many times since he had learned how to unloose them he had practised the art, and the art remained. With his hands on his knees, the chain between them, he looked like a prisoner in irons, but he could release himself at any moment.

'Do I look all right?' he repeated.

'Of course, dear Father, you always look all right.'

As the sound of the warder's footsteps, between their five minutes' interval, died away, he gave his daughter a meaning look and twitched his shrunken wrists and claw-thin fingers which the handcuffs no longer held.

Their eyes met: she understood what he meant.

Rudy pulled down the sleeves of his worn-out jacket; he thought of the days when it had served him in awkward moments; reinforced by his daughter's physical help, his being knew what to do in case of a fight. He had had many fights in his day; he knew where to plant the blows, he knew where the pressure-points were—under the elbow, behind the shoulders, in the groin, and he memorised them, while he and Angela were talking.

'Time for you to go, Madam,' said the gaoler, opening the door.

Rudy didn't wait. At the sound of the gaoler's footsteps nearing stealthily, he had unleashed his hands, and the gaoler, taken utterly by surprise, was lying sprawled, his face hidden by his crash-helmet, motionless, his eyes adrift, on the stone floor.

'Follow me,' said Angela.

Rudy followed her through devious ways where no one challenged them, for every prison has its times off, to a small door beyond which stood a car. Angela's car. They got in and drove away.

Rudy fell asleep; but waking up he asked, not knowing where, or even who he was,

'How did you know the way?'

'Don't ask me,' she said accelerating. 'I've been that way before, more than once.'

Her tone told him something, but not everything; and trying to solve the puzzle, he dropped off to sleep again.

For most of the time Rudy was asleep; he woke up when he saw lights flashing, then he dropped off again.

*

After a few hours they stopped abruptly, and Rudy, waking from his half-dream, said 'Where are we?'

'At the frontier,' Angela replied. 'It's quite all right, Father, I've got your passport, the bearded one,' she laughed, 'which looks quite like you, at least as you used to be.'

Rudy could hardly take in what she was saying, but the customs official seemed satisfied. Rudy, lurching, opening and closing his eyes, couldn't take in what was happening.

Then they were off again, for an hour or more, and it was dark before they arrived.

Angela had to help him out of the car for he wasn't steady on his feet, and didn't know which door to get out of, hers or his, or how to open it.

'Where are we?' he asked.

'Oh, a long way away,' she answered, still carefully lending him her arm. 'They won't find us here. Besides, it's another country. Don't you remember the customs?'

Dimly he did, but though his eyes kept closing, he still remembered, subconsciously, the dangers attaching to a life like his, and the dangers they might involve for other people.

'Is this your house?' he asked, still accepting her aid towards the unlighted windows.

'And will your husband—I can't remember his name—mind? And you have the baby—' He spoke as if the baby might mind, too.

'Oh no, the baby is quite happy. He's asleep now, at least I hope so. And Jacko knows all about it (now). He isn't here at the moment, but he's in sympathy with you, otherwise I couldn't have done—well, what I did do.'

Still, Rudy wasn't quite convinced, and the seven devils who enter in when one has been expelled, began to raise their heads.

'Shall I sleep in the garage? I shall be quite comfortable there, or in that hut in the garden—' Tired as he was he had an instinct for the precautions he ought to take.

Angela opened the front door.

'I shall be bitterly offended,' she said, 'if you sleep anywhere but in the house. And so will Jacko. Your bed is aired—everything is laid on. Now what would you like for supper—a mixed grill, an omelette? or what?—An appetiser of course to start with. There are plenty of them,'—she waved towards the sideboard, where the bottles gleamed, whisky, gin, vodka, each with its special appeal, its message of encouragement to the weary human race. 'Or would you like something else, another sort of cocktail?'

'I would like you,' he said, and before she had time to assent or dissent he had clasped her in his arms. Gently she released herself, and bared her bosom to him for the last time.

PAINS AND PLEASURES

THERE is always room for improvement, but there is not always time for it. Henry Kitson had reached and over-reached the allotted span. In his youth he had been something of a teleologist. An immense and varied field of ambition lay open to him. He would become one with his desires; he would achieve an important and worthwhile aim in which his whole self, all the contents of his personality, such as they were, would be completely and forever expressed.

These aims took different forms. He would climb the Matterhorn (in those days a considerable feat) and, if he had known about it, he would have wanted to climb the North face of the Eiger. He would also play the 'Moonlight Sonata' quite perfectly: the last movement would have no terrors for him. Adding to these achievements he would learn to read, and to speak, at least five languages; his Aunt Patsy, his father's eldest sister, had done so, so why not he? He would reduce his handicap at golf which was 12, to scratch or even to plus something. He would write a book (he couldn't decide on what subject) that would be a classic, immortal: the name of Henry Kitson would resound down the ages.

And he had other ambitions.

Alas, none of them had materialised, and here he was, in the early seventies, with nothing to show for them. He was comfortably off, with a pension from the firm in the City who had employed him for nearly half a century, and with the money he had saved up—for he had not, mentally, grown old with the years; he was not, and could not be, 'his age'; he still regarded himself as the impecunious, ambitious young man he was at twenty-five.

Apart from the tendency which often overtakes elderly men to regard himself as penniless, his situation was most fortunate. He had, as general factotum, a retired policeman, who cleaned his cottage, cooked his meals and drove his car. Wilson ('Bill' to Henry Kitson) was perfect: he did everything he should, and nothing he shouldn't. In this he was very different from some of his predecessors, who had done everything they shouldn't, and nothing that they should.

Coming at the tail-end of this procession of mainly unsatisfactory characters ('character' was a word used in the old days, but in a different sense, when a prospective employer was asking for a reference) Bill had, of course, for Henry, an overwhelming advantage. After many years of domestic darkness, Bill was the light. Whenever Henry thought of him he gave (if he could remember to) thanksgiving to Heaven for Bill.

At the same time it was a great temptation, as it always is if the opportunity arises, to flog the willing horse. Bill, like Barkis, was willing; and Henry sometimes asked him to do jobs that he would never have dared to ask of any of Bill's less amenable forerunners.

With the advent of Bill, 'a soundless calm', in Emily Brontë's words, descended on Henry. Domestic troubles were over; nothing to resent; nothing to fight against; no sense of Sisyphus bearing an unbearable weight uphill. No grievance at all. Had he lived by his grievances, was a question that Henry sometimes asked himself. Had his resistance to them, his instinct to fight back and assert himself and show what he was made of, somehow strengthened his hold on life, and prolonged it?

Now he had nothing to resist. What Bill did with his spare time—if he occupied it, as Henry suspected, at the pub and the betting-shop, was no business of his. As far as he was concerned, Bill could do no wrong.

But just as someone who has always carried a weight on his shoulders, or on his mind or on his heart and who is suddenly relieved of it, feels in himself a void, an incentive to living suddenly taken away, even so Henry, lacking this incentive, found his life empty, almost purposeless.

Gratitude to Bill was his major preoccupation, but how to express it? Bill was by no means indifferent to money—he liked it and he knew more about it than Henry, with a lifetime's experience of business, did.

Little presents, Bill was not averse to them; but they didn't represent to Henry even a small part of his indebtedness to Bill. Perhaps a bonus of ten per cent for honesty?

Undoubtedly, Henry Kitson's retired and retiring life was the happier for Bill's presence, and for his presents to Bill, but it was also the emptier, now that his grievance had been taken away. Most people need something to live against, and if this objective, positive or negative, is removed, they suffer for it. Henry had friends in the neighbourhood whom he saw as often as he could; but they did not supply him with that extra-personal incentive—

'Live with one aim, but let that aim be high'—or low—which he had had when X, and Y, and Z were ill-treating him, and whose malfeasances, he felt, must be resisted to the ultimate extent of his emotional if not his personal prowess.

With Bill in charge of his domestic affairs, there was nothing at all to be resisted, nothing to aim at—for Bill was a placid, self-contained character, who had seen a lot of the ups and downs of life, and had little to learn from it which Henry, with the best will in the world, could supply.

So his life stratified itself into a routine, pleasant but nearly featureless. There were, however, two features in his day which had an emotional content and significance, and to which he clung, for they represented what he liked, and what he disliked: as long as he stuck to them and could look forward to or dread them, he knew he was keeping the advance of senility at bay.

One was concerned with Bill. Bill in common with many other men, rich and poor, criminal and honest, liked a drink: and Henry saw to it that Bill's 'elevenses' should be a tot of whisky. With all the variations of vocal expression at his command, he would ask Bill if he would like a drink; and Bill, with all the variations of expression at his command, would say 'Yes'. From the time when he was called, at 8 o'clock, Henry looked forward to this little episode. At the word 'drink' Bill's dark eyes would glow, like coals that had suddenly been set alight. 'Good health!' he would say, before he took his glass into the kitchen. Henry never failed to get pleasure from this simple interchange of amenities, just as he never failed to get pain from the other cardinal event of his day, and unfortunately he had longer to anticipate it. This was to put out his cat, Ginger, at bed time. He was fond of Ginger, but Ginger was old and set in his ways, and did not like being put out. Being a neuter, he did not have the same motive that many cats have for prowling about at night, growling and yowling and keeping everyone within earshot awake. He wanted to be warm and comfortable; and although there was a shed and an outhouse in the garden which he must have known about, he preferred Henry's fireside, and when Henry opened the garden door to put him out he would streak past through Henry's legs and sit down in front of the fire, purring loudly and triumphantly.

Henry found this daily or rather nightly ejection of Ginger very painful; but it was inevitable, for with age he had lost whatever house-training he ever had, and misbehaved accordingly. It fell to Bill's lot to deal with these misdemeanours, which always happened in a certain place, on some stone flags by the cellar-door. Perhaps Ginger thought that his oblations would be more acceptable there than anywhere else; and as someone said, 'it is impossible to make a cat understand that it should do what you want it to do.'

When bed-time approached, Henry picked Ginger up and carried him towards the garden-door, the fatal exit. Then Ginger would purr ingratiatingly, as though to say, 'You can't have the heart to do this.' Sometimes, in rebellious moods, he would struggle and claw and scratch: but the end was always the same; he made a desperate dash to get back into the house. Often the hateful process had to be repeated more than once and Henry peering through the glass door (which he couldn't resist doing) would see Ginger's amber eyes fixed on him with a look of heart-rending reproach.

Henry knew what the correct solution was: *he* should clean up the mess that Ginger made, and not leave it to Bill. But how tempting it is to flog the willing horse! And if ever he yielded to Ginger's protests, whether in the form of purr or scratch, and let him stay indoors, he refrained from asking Bill what had happened outside the cellar-door.

Not that Bill ever complained. When Henry surreptitiously went down to the cellar-door and saw and smelt the unmistakeable traces (however carefully cleaned up) of Ginger's nightly defecations, not a word was said between them.

But as time passed, and the pension-supported Henry came to rely more and more on his daily routine of living, with nothing to jerk him out of it, the problem of pleasure and pain, as exemplified by Bill's whisky elevenses in the morning, and Ginger's compulsory expulsions at night, began to assume undue importance. Henry simply did not *want* his septuagenarian happiness to depend on these two absurd poles of emotional comfort and discomfort.

What *could* he do? Human beings were (so it was generally thought), more valuable and more important than dumb animals (a ridiculous expression, for many animals including Ginger were far from dumb). Certainly Bill was much more valuable to him than Ginger was: Bill was an asset of the highest order whereas Ginger (except for Henry's affection for him) was merely a debit. He was very greedy; he did nothing to earn his keep; he could not, and did not try, to catch the most unsophisticated mouse; he was just a liability and a parasite.

Bill, though such a mild-mannered man, must in his time have been a tough character, and used to dealing with tough characters, criminals, murderers and such, as policemen have to be.

*

'I wish I knew what to do about Ginger,' Henry said. 'He makes such a fuss when I turn him out at night. But you know better than I do I'm sorry to say,' (and Henry was genuinely sorry) 'what happens when he stays indoors. It's not his fault, he doesn't mean it, he can't help it, but well, there it is.'

'I know what you refer to, sir,' said the ex-policeman with an instinctive delicacy of utterance, 'and I think I know the solution. Indeed, I have been turning it over in my mind for some time. It's really quite simple.'

'You mean it would be simple to have Ginger put down?'

'Oh no, sir,' said Bill, horrified. 'Nothing as drastic as that. Ginger is a good old cat, he wouldn't hurt a mouse.' (This was only too true.) 'I am attached to him, just as you are, and when I said the solution is quite simple, it *is* quite simple, if you know what I mean.'

'I'm not sure that I do. What *is* the solution?'

'Just this, sir. Give him a box with sawdust in it, and put it where he usually—where he usually does his business, if you know what I mean—and I'll show it to him and then if he doesn't understand at *once*—but he *will*, all cats do. I'll put his paw in it, and he will soon know what it's for—and, and act accordingly.'

'What an excellent idea,' said Henry, a little patronisingly. 'I wonder that I never thought of it. There is an empty seed-box in the greenhouse, I think, that would be just right for the purpose. And sawdust I suppose is quite easy to get hold of.'

'Well, not all that easy, sir,' said Bill. 'But having in mind the ash-tree that fell down, which I am cutting up for firewood, it shouldn't be difficult, in fact I've got nearly enough already.'

'Thank you very much, Bill.'

Ginger was duly introduced to the box, and his paw gently embedded in the sawdust. This he took very well, purring all the time; but when the ceremony of initiation was over, he did not use the box for its intended cloacal purpose, but settled down in it, with his fore-paws tucked under him, and his tail neatly curled round his flank, and went to sleep.

Next day he was discovered still asleep in the sawdust box, but alas, only a few inches away were the extremely malodorous vestiges of Ginger's digestion or indigestion, which the box had been intended to absorb.

'Never mind,' said Bill, 'he'll learn in time.'

But Ginger didn't learn. He spent many hours, sometimes all

day, slumbering on his sawdust mattress, purring to himself, no
doubt, instead of sitting in front of Henry's comfortable fireplace
purring to *him*.

'I'm afraid Ginger isn't going to learn, Bill,' said Henry.

'It looks like not,' said Bill. 'You can't teach an old cat new
tricks.' He laughed at this sally. 'But we can give him a few days
grace.'

*

The few days passed, but Ginger did not learn. He still regarded
the sawdust box as his bed; and like a well-conducted person, he
did not wish to pollute it. It was woundingly evident that he still
preferred it to Henry's fireside and that his adjacent loo was very
convenient to him.

Henry knew that he himself ought to undo what Ginger had
done; but somehow he couldn't bring himself to. 'I am over
seventy,' he reasoned, 'and why should I sacrifice myself to the
selfish whims of a cat, especially when it has been given every
opportunity to satisfy the needs of Nature in other ways?' All the
same, he didn't relish the nightly ordeal of turning Ginger out.

'I'm afraid our experiment with Ginger hasn't been successful,' he said to Bill. 'He goes on making a nuisance of himself. I
wonder if *you* would mind putting him out at night? He doesn't
like it, he claws and clutches at me, but I dare say that with you
he would be more—more sensible. Would you mind?'

'Of course not, Mr. Kitson,' replied Bill, who when he remembered, preferred to call Henry 'Mr. Kitson' rather than 'sir'.

*

Days passed; Henry saw little of Ginger, so content was he on his
sawdust bed that he didn't bother to visit Henry in the sitting-
room. Henry caught fleeting glimpses of him in the garden, tail-
twitching, intent on birds which he was far too old to catch. 'Blast
him!' thought Henry. 'Ungrateful beast!'

One day there was a knock at his study door. 'Come in!' said
Henry, who had always asked people not to knock. 'Come in!
Who is it?'

'Oh, *Bill*!' he exclaimed, instantly welcoming. 'What can I do for you?'

He hadn't noticed how upset and how unlike himself Bill looked.

'It's like this, sir,' Bill began and stopped.

'Like what, Bill?' asked Henry, and his heart turned over with a presage of disaster.

'It's like this,' Bill paused, and repeated more slowly and with a note of authority in his voice that reminded Henry that he had once been a policeman, 'It's like this.'

'Like what?' Henry asked again.

'It's like this,' Bill said, and he looked taller under the top-light of Henry's study, and almost as if he was wearing uniform, 'I want to give in my notice. I want to ask for my stamps.'

'But *why*, Bill?' Henry asked, aghast.

'Well, Mr. Kitson, you may think it silly of me, but it's because of Ginger.'

'Because of Ginger?' Again Henry's heart smote him. 'You mean because of the messes he still makes?'

'Oh no, Mr. Kitson. I don't mind them at all. They're all in the day's work, if you know what I mean.'

'Then what *do* you mind?'

'I mind putting him out at night, sir. He claws and clutches and scratches me—you wouldn't believe it. Not that I'd mind with a human being, I've had plenty of people to deal with much worse than he is—after all, he's only got his claws, and I think he's lost most of his teeth, but all the same, I don't like it, sir, and that's why I'm giving in my notice and asking for my cards.'

Henry was not too distraught to ignore the dignity of Bill's resignation.

'What will you do now, Bill?' he asked.

'Oh, well, sir, I shall find something. There are jobs waiting for a single man. I'm not a single man, really, I'm a widower, which is the nearest thing, and I have no ties. I haven't put an advert in the paper yet, but I shall find a job you may be sure.'

Henry, too, was sure he would find another job; but where

would he find another Bill? It was all too wretched, but he knew men of Bill's type and they didn't change their minds easily once they were made up.

'Listen!' he said loudly, as if Bill was deaf. 'I don't mind cleaning up the mess that Ginger leaves and I don't mind putting him out at night. I know the way he claws and scratches, but I thought that with you who feeds him, he would behave better than he does with me. It seems that he hasn't, and I am very sorry, Bill, but I shall be only too glad to take him on, eating, sleeping, and whatever else he wants to do—and relieve you of the responsibility.' (Just as Ginger relieves *himself*, he thought but did not say.)

'I couldn't ask you to do that, sir. You have been very good to me, but I shall find a job where there aren't any animals to work for.'

At this rather ungracious remark Henry Kitson groaned again.

'I know I ought not to have left the dirty work to you, Bill,' he said, with the belated contrition that most people feel at one time or another. 'I know I shouldn't have, and if you agree to stay I'll be responsible for everything to do with Ginger, by day or by night.'

'Oh no, sir, I couldn't let you do that, a gentleman in your position. And in any case, it isn't *that* that I mind.'

Henry groaned again. He was utterly at a loss.

'Then what *do* you mind, Bill?'

'I mind putting him out at night, Mr. Kitson. He creates so, you wouldn't believe it, but yes, you would, you've had it so often yourself. It isn't his scratching and miauling I mind, it's when he purrs and tries to pretend I'm doing him a kindness. I'm not that tender-hearted, but I know what it's like to spend a night in the open,' the ex-policeman added.

Henry's eyes grew moist.

'Well, I'll put him out tonight.'

'Oh no, Mr. Kitson, I'll see to him.'

But Henry displayed unexpected firmness.

'No, no, let's leave him indoors. And if anything happens, I'll take care of it.'

'Very good, sir,' said Bill, smartly. 'Good night, sir,' he added, on a note of finality that echoed through the room when he was gone.

*

Ginger was lying in front of the fire, on one of his rare visits to Henry's study since he had yielded to the superior attractions of the sawdust box. He purred, as he always did when Henry so much as looked at him. Every now and then he stretched out his paw, as though trying to make himself more comfortable than he already was. Every now and then he half opened his eyes and looked at Henry with what Henry called his 'beatific' expression, suggesting his mysterious but not unkindly insight into the past, the present, and the future.

'I won't disturb him,' Henry thought, turning out the light, 'let him stay here if he wants to; and if he prefers the cellar-door he knows the way.'

At eight o'clock the next morning Bill appeared as usual, bringing Henry's early-morning tea. He drew the curtains.

'There it is!' he said.

Henry had heard this aubade before, but he was always foxed by it.

'Where is what?' he asked.

'The day,' said Bill.

Henry, nursing again his discomfiture at not having foreseen this obvious answer, sat up and looked out of the window. It was a dreary November day, but Bill didn't seem uncheerful.

'I'm afraid I've some bad news for you,' he said.

Henry tried to collect his waking thoughts. A pall enveloped them. How could Bill be so unkind?

'I suppose you mean that you are leaving?' he said, stretching out his hand for the teapot.

'Oh no, Mr. Kitson, it's much worse than that.'

'What can be worse?' thought Henry miserably, and uttered his thought out loud. 'What can be worse, Bill?'

'It's much worse,' said Bill.

Eight o'clock in the morning is not the best time to receive bad news, and especially if one doesn't know what it is. Henry relinquished the teapot and sank back on the pillow.

'Tell me,' he said.

'Well, Mr. Kitson,' said Bill, with his back to the light, while he was arranging Henry's clothes on a chair, 'to tell you the truth—'

'Oh, do tell me, Bill.'

'To tell you the *truth*,' Bill repeated, as if one sort of truth was more valuable than another, 'Ginger is dead.'

'Good God,' said Henry, who had envisaged some cosmic nuclear disturbance especially aimed at him. 'Good God!' he repeated, with intense relief. And then he remembered Ginger last night, sitting on the hearth-rug and purring loudly whenever Henry vouchsafed a look at him. 'Poor Ginger!' he said.

'Yes, sir, and I feel very sorry about him too. Ginger was a good old cat. Would you like to see him, Mr. Kitson?'

'What, now?'

'Now, or any time. He's there, he isn't far away.'

Henry got out of bed. He put on his dressing-gown and followed Bill downstairs.

'The usual place,' said Bill.

It was dark down there, so they turned on the light. Ginger was lying in his sawdust box, looking quite comfortable and life-like, except that his head seemed to be twisted over.

Henry stooped down and stroked his cold fur and half listened for the purr that didn't come; then he led the way upstairs.

'He seemed so well last night,' he said to Bill.

'Oh yes, sir, but animals are like that, just like human beings, if you know what I mean. Here today and gone tomorrow.'

Henry felt the bitter sensation of loss that we are all bound to feel at one time or another.

'But he seemed so well last night,' he repeated.

'Yes,' replied Bill, 'but he was very old. We all have to go sometime.'

An unworthy suspicion stirred in Henry's mind, but he stifled it.

'And now I've got to lose you, too, Bill,' he said.

'Oh no, sir,' said Bill, promptly. 'I've thought it over, and I don't want to go, that is, unless you want me to.'

A wave of relief—there was no other word for it—swept over Henry.

'Please stay,' he said, 'please stay, Bill.'

'Yes, I will, Mr. Kitson,' Bill answered and there was a surge and an uplift in his voice. 'We've got cutlets for lunch—will that be all right?'

His pronunciation was rather odd, and he made it sound like 'catlets'.

*

'Would you like a drink now, Bill?' Henry asked. 'Or is it too early?'

'I won't say no,' said Bill, and the light began to glow behind his coal-black eyes.

PLEASE DO NOT TOUCH

VIVIAN VOSPER was a bachelor who lived alone in a very small mews house but in a burglarious part of London. All parts of London are burglarious to some extent, but this one was particularly so. Twice his house had been burgled, and the second time he had been beaten up and tied up by some masked men and had only managed to wriggle himself free from his bonds after an hour or more of skin-abrasive effort and a great deal of physical and nervous discomfort. The police, when he was able to summon them, were very kind and helpful as they always are; they asked him if he was suffering from shock, and he said No, but he was wrong, for no sooner had they left, promising to do their best to find the culprits, than he was seized by uncontrollable shivers, and felt obliged to call in his doctor in the early hours of the morning, a thing he had never done before.

He survived, however, and he hadn't lost much of value for he hadn't much of value to lose; chiefly the drinks he kept on the sideboard, to which the thieves had liberally helped themselves, before relieving themselves, as in the habit of burglars, all over his sitting-room floor. With the help of his daily help, who came at eight o'clock in the morning, he cleared up the mess; but the material stink of it, no less than the indescribable smell of violation that any burglary brings, remained with him for several days.

Then there was all the bother of applying to the insurance company for the value of the articles he had lost, not only the bottles of drink, so expensive nowadays—but silver, and vases, and trinkets.

But though he hadn't much minded the first burglary—indeed he was in bed and asleep when it happened and didn't know about it until the morning—he did mind the second, with its violence and its sequel of nervous shock, not to mention the loss of objects that he treasured; and like the hero of Poe's story, 'The Cask of Amontillado', he vowed revenge.

It was the story that gave him his idea, for though he had no cask of Amontillado and no cellar to wall up the miscreants, or the 'villains' as the police sometimes called them—such a quaint old-fashioned word—supposing he had been able to; he had a few bottles of Amontillado sherry which would serve as a bait. He would doctor them; but how, and with what?

As a butterfly-collector many years ago (he was now over sixty) he still had a small phial of cyanide of potassium to refresh (if that was the word) the evaporating supply in the white plaster-of-Paris basis of his killing-bottle. In those far-off days you could obtain the stuff simply by signing the chemist's poison-book; but there was enough of it left to account for several gangs of burglars.

It was so long since he had given up butterfly-collecting and moth-collecting. For some reason he preferred moths to butter-flies. Not only because there were so many more of them—two or three thousand compared with a mere seventy species of butter-flies. True, some of the moths were very dreary; there was the Wainscot family, the Footman family, each member of those two families being almost indistinguishable from the other and only of interest in their slightly varied drabness to experts of whom Vivian had never professed to be one.

On the other hand, some of the moths were very exciting. The Oak Eggar, for instance, with its strange capacity (radar-inspired no doubt) for attracting a husband or a wife from many miles away; there were the tiger-moths, so decorative; there was the lappet moth (lasciocampa quercifolia) which Vivian had never succeeded in capturing. And the puss-moths, dear creatures, with their green caterpillars, aggressive and hostile in demeanour, but with their soft silken tongues making impenetrable chrysalis little fortresses out of the hard bark of a poplar tree.

And the hawk-moths of course, all the hawk-moths. More than

once it had been Vivian's good fortune to capture the Convolvulus Hawk Moth (sphinx convulvuli), that rare visitant; but never, in spite of diligent study of the potato fields had he ever discovered either the larva or the imago (as they called the perfect insect) of the Death's Head (acherontia atropos) both of which were said to squeak, if disturbed.

Looking at the little poison-bottle, so long disused, he thought of these creatures (now, thanks to chemicals, much rarer than they used to be) which he had loved and yet had doomed to an untimely death, stretched out on a setting-board, the wings that had borne them so freely through the air pinned down at an un- natural angle, and when released from the bondage of the stretching-board transferred to another more elegant mauso- leum.

They had died painlessly, of that he was sure; a slight flutter- ing of wings over the poison-drenched plaster, and all was over. When at one time he had sealed their fate with an infusion, an exhalation of chopped-up laurel leaves, it had been more linger- ing.

They had done him no harm, no harm at all, and as he thought of their poor bodies slowly decaying under glass-covered shelves in a cabinet which neither he nor any one else looked at, he did not feel happy with himself.

But the burglars *had* done him harm; they had not only robbed him and beaten him up and pinioned him as if he was a moth on a stretching-board, they had callously left him to get free as best he could, or to die if he couldn't. 'Ye are of more importance than many sparrows' Christ had said; and Vivian persuaded himself that he was of more importance than many moths.

He uncorked the little bottle, and cautiously, very cautiously, sniffed its contents. Yes, there it was, that almond-breathing, aromatic, but lethal smell. He snatched his nose away. Better be on the safe side. The moths and butterflies, poor creatures, hadn't been able to snatch their noses or probosces away; they had the stopper of the bottle clamped down on them.

Vivian's mind went over these old memories, from the time when he thought it was almost a personal triumph to insert a crimson-underwing, its helpless wings held tightly between his fingers, into the lethal chamber, a miniature forecast of the gas-chambers employed by Hitler.

'Why am I doing this?' he asked himself as, with the cyanide safely stoppered, he advanced towards the elegant, festive, festive, cheer-inducing bottle of Amontillado. 'Why am I doing it? Is it like me to do it? I have never wanted to hurt anyone before—except a few insects, and I never thought I was *hurting* them, only *collecting* them, as so many naturalists have. Has my nature changed? Have I become a different person just because a few bandits from whom half the people I know, people with far more precious things to lose, have suffered more than I have? Would it not be better,' he asked himself, still with the half empty little bottle in his hand, as he approached the big brim-full bottle of Amontillado, 'to forget all about it? If it is true, as they now say, that violence is inherent in human nature, who am I to resent being its victim? I mean'—he hastily corrected himself—'to resent suffering from it at the hands of other people? Of course if I'—and he looked down at the innocent-looking poison—'were to *retaliate*, it wouldn't be *violence*, it would just illustrate the well-known law that every action has an equal and consequent reaction.'

He took the bottle of sherry and uncorked it. Better drink a glass, he thought, that way it will look more natural. He enjoyed the drink; what a pity (for now his sense of behaving unlike himself was taking the upper hand) to spoil such good wine. Yet spoilt it must be or else—he couldn't finish the sentence even to himself. He took the little bottle—how small it was compared with the big one—and decanted from it into its large neighbour a fragrant tablespoonful, then corked both bottles up.

It's all nonsense, he told himself, it's just a joke. In the morning I shall feel quite different and empty both the bottles down the drain; but in the meanwhile it would be safer to take precautions.

Having written on a stick-on label, in the largest capital letters, 'PLEASE DO NOT TOUCH' he affixed it to the sherry bottle, which he placed in a prominent position on his drink-table so that neither by day nor night could its warning notice be ignored.

He went to bed but not to sleep, for his nervous constitution being unaccustomed to the idea of such a violent emotion as vengeance, avenged itself on him with an attack of acute indigestion, so acute that he wondered if he might not in some moment of misadventure—perhaps when he was decanting the cyanide into the sherry-bottle—have touched the fatal fluid with his finger and 'despatched his finger travelling to his nob,' as Meredith once said—meaning, he touched his head. And from his head it was only a matter of inches to his mouth, and then—

Two or three times during the night he got up and went downstairs into his sitting-room, where he kept the drinks, just to make sure that the bottle was in place, that no mouse, for instance, had nibbled at its cork, for since his butterfly collecting days Vivian had become almost a Buddhist in his dislike of taking life. No, it was untouched and apparently unfingered, though it had begun to assert its presence as if it were the only object in the room. At length, after a dangerously large dose of barbiturates, he went to sleep.

Next morning he woke with the usual sense of presentiment and inability to face the day. As a rule this wore off when he was up and about; but today it lingered. He must offer some explanation of this bottle to his daily help.

'Ethel,' he said, 'have there been any more rats here just lately?'

'Yes, sir,' she answered promptly, 'there was quite a big one in the kitchen and it scared me stiff. These old houses, they breed rats. Ever since I've been with you, sir, these rats have been about, and in my opinion they breed here, down in the basement, where we never go, for it's a darksome place and not nice to go into. If I wasn't that attached to you, sir, I should have given in my notice long ago, for if there's anything I hate, it's rats. And most people feel as I do.'

'I don't like them myself,' said Vivian, looking nervously round the room. 'They give you the creeps, don't they? And they are so artful, almost like burglars.'

'Yes, sir, and as I've often said before, you ought to put down some poison for them. I know it isn't a nice thing to do, but they aren't nice, either. In my flat, which is a modern flat, not like this old place, which may be picturesque but isn't healthy, we don't have rats. If we did, I doubt if any of the tenants who value cleanliness would stay.'

Vivian saw an opening here.

'Well, as a matter of fact, Ethel, I've been thinking over what you said and I had an idea. I've had some poison in my medicine cupboard for many years.' He explained why. 'Now I've put some of it in this bottle of sherry'—he held the bottle up for her to see —'because I believe rats are very partial to sherry.'

'I've never heard that, sir, but they'll eat or drink anything that a human being wouldn't touch.'

Again he held the bottle up for her inspection.

'I've labelled it "Please don't touch." Rats wouldn't understand that'—he gave a little laugh—'but sometimes when we're both out of the house people do come in, window-cleaners, electricians, and such-like—Mr. Stanforth, a few doors away, has the keys, and I trust him absolutely. You know him, don't you?'

'Oh yes, sir, he's an old friend. It was through him I came to you.'

'I'm grateful to him for that, and for many other kindnesses. But what I wanted to say was someone might come into the house with the best of intentions, and seeing this bottle they might be tempted—one shouldn't put temptation into people's way—to have a swig. So I labelled it, "Please don't touch".'

'I'm not sure if that would stop them, sir.'

Vivian saw the point of this.

'There are other bottles'—he waved to four or five—'that they could dip into. Meanwhile, shall we lay a trap for the rats? And if so, where?'

'In the kitchen, I think. That's where they like to come to pick up what they can—not that I ever leave any food lying about. But they have a nose for whatever isn't meant for them.'

'A saucer, do you think? Anything as long as it doesn't poison you or me.'

'I know exactly what, sir. That little Chinese bowl, it won't spill over, however hard they try.'

'Well, take the bottle, Ethel, and we'll see what happens. But be very careful. Hold your breath while you're putting the stuff in.'

She smiled at his scrupulosity, and presently returned with the bottle, its contents diminished by an eighth.

*

Vivian couldn't cook for himself, except a breakfast egg which Ethel generally cooked for him. For his main meals he went out to his club, to which he invited friends, if he had not been lucky enough to be invited by them. Otherwise he lunched or dined alone, in solitary state.

Sometimes, however, he went into the kitchen in case there was some tit-bit that Ethel had bought for him which didn't need cooking. He rather enjoyed these exploratory visits to the fridge. But today—the day of the rat-hunt—having been asked out to dinner, he lunched at his club and didn't go into the kitchen.

The next morning, after a better night than the last, he was greeted by Ethel with a radiant face.

'Do you know what's happened, sir?'

Vivian was mystified.

'No.'

'Would you like to see?'

Vivian, having no idea what he was going to see, said 'Yes, of course.'

After a short interval the door opened and Ethel appeared, with glowing face, holding by its tail an enormous rat, cat-like in size.

'I found it this morning, sir, close by the bowl. It must have been thirsty, because the bowl was half empty, but it couldn't get any further because the poison had done its work. It didn't suffer at all, so you needn't think about that. I'm going to show it to the man what collects the garbage and ask him if he's ever seen such a big one. But I think we ought to put some more sherry in the bowl, in case another comes along.'

The next morning another rodent sherry-addict did come along, and suffered the same fate as its predecessor; it wasn't quite so large, but suspended by its tail it made a considerable impression on Vivian, reclining on his bed.

For two or three days there were no more rodent casualties, and then appeared another larger than the other two.

'They're the talk of the whole mews,' Ethel said. 'Everyone here has rats in one way or another, and they all want to know how you get rid of them. I told them you had a secret, but I wouldn't tell them what it was, sir, even if I knew, without your permission. It's something he puts into a bottle, I said. I wouldn't be surprised if Mr. Stanforth himself came round and asked you —he's that plagued by rats. I didn't say you would be prepared to tell him, sir, because it's a trade secret, as you might say, and you're no professional rat-catcher. But he was most insistent.'

Mr. Stanforth had a flat in one of the mews houses, and was a very useful and valued member of the little street, because most of his neighbours entrusted their door-keys to him, so that if they lost them, as sometimes happened, he was prepared to let them in, at any hour, or if a tradesman called with goods to deliver, or the postman with a parcel when there was no one at home to receive it, Mr. Stanforth took charge and in due course restored the errant object to its owner.

Having been there twenty years he was known to nearly all the residents, most of whom availed themselves of his services, for which he charged no fee but received enough in tips handsomely to augment his pension.

And not only did he know the residents, he knew by name or by sight many of the visitors, many of the tradesmen who served them, and all their daily helps, if they had any. He was in fact a mine of information; he knew far more about everyone in the street than they knew about each other; and being an ex-policeman he had a keen eye for any stranger, especially any suspicious-looking stranger, who invaded its precincts. At the same time he was no night-watchman, and since many burglars, though by no means all, operate by night, he had not been able to detect who were the miscreants who had twice broken into Vivian's house. He did, however, tell Vivian, with whom he was on friendly terms, that he had a clue and was following it up, 'It could have been somebody who knew your house,' he said rather darkly, 'because after they had trussed you up they seemed to know where to look for everything, they got away that quick, or so you told me, Mr. Vosper.'

'You are quite right,' said Vivian, remembering with renewed bitterness the long silence that had followed while he was trying, sometimes hopefully, sometimes despairingly—to release himself from his bonds. 'But I haven't any friends who are burglars.'

'You never know nowadays,' said Mr. Stanforth, 'you never know. Now what was it you wanted to see me about?'

Vivian had almost forgotten why he had telephoned to Mr. Stanforth, asking him to look in if he had a moment to spare.

He looked round his sitting-room, hoping to be reminded.

'Oh, it was this,' he said, taking the sherry-bottle, and holding it up for Mr. Stanforth's inspection. 'It contains some stuff I use to poison the rats.'

Mr. Stanforth's eyes brightened as he took the bottle from Vivian's outstretched hand.

'Of course I've heard about it, sir,' he said excitedly. 'We've all heard about it, and how you've used it to get rid of a dozen rats.'

'Well, not a dozen, but five or six.'

Mr. Stanforth looked disappointed at this reduced number of casualties. 'They're a perfect pest in these old-time dwellings. I suffer from them myself, so I know.' With his hand on the cork he asked, 'Can I take a sniff, sir?'

'Yes,' said Vivian, 'but careful, careful, it's rather dangerous, so I put this on it'—and he pointed to the label, PLEASE DO NOT TOUCH,—'in case someone should come in while I'm out, and be tempted to take a swig. You mustn't put temptation into people's way. You Mr. Stanforth know who can be trusted and who can't, but present company excepted, we all fall into temptation sometimes, especially working-men who get thirsty delivering goods—'

'Oh yes, Mr. Vosper, I know what you mean.'

'You keep tabs on them, as far as you can, but you can't be answerable for everyone, so I thought I'd just tell you.'

'Quite right, sir, and I'll drop a hint where I think it might be useful.' He paused. 'You haven't got the recipe, sir? There are quite a lot of our neighbours, not to mention me, who are plagued with rats, and I'm sometimes asked, "How does Mr. Vosper get rid of his?".'

Vivian hesitated before he explained. 'But the cyanide is hard to get hold of in these days. It happened I had some by me from when I was a butterfly-collector. Chemists are pretty strict about it now. But there's no harm in trying.'

'I'll remember that, sir. You don't mind if I mention this to some of the others who are plagued by rats?'

'Oh no, Mr. Stanforth, but just warn them that the stuff is dangerous.'

*

Days passed and nothing happened to disturb the harmony of Rateable House (as Vivian's dwelling was bitterly called). No more rats; doubtless, being the most intelligent of animals, with an instinct for survival which we have lost, they had informed their fellows that Rateable House was a place to be avoided. No more scratching and scurrying behind the wainscot; no more wondering if it was a rat or a mouse, or something less tangible but more horrid.

The disappearance of the rats had one effect which Vivian didn't know whether to regret or not: it had taken away Ethel's one subject of conversation. Sometimes she forgot and began, 'If it wasn't for those awful rats—' and then, remembering they no longer existed, fell into an offended silence, as if their absence was an even greater grievance than their presence. 'Those rats,' she once said enigmatically, 'did help to keep burglars away.'

'How do you mean, Ethel?'

'Well, most burglars are frightened of rats, just as you and I are.'

'So they may be, but they can't tell from outside if there are rats inside.'

'They have their own ways of finding out. Rats and burglars are much the same, as you should know, sir. They're both thieves, and they pass on information to each other, we don't know how.'

Soon she discovered new causes of complaint, irregularities in what she felt should be Vivian's fixed routine—clothes omitted from the laundry basket, objects mislaid which had cost her much time, and much waste of time, to track down. But these were only ruffles on the smooth surface of their relationship, protests, demonstrations against his taking her services too much for granted. And more than once she said, 'I will say this, Mr. Vivian, you got rid of those rats, which is more than most of us can do.'

Vivian thought the matter over, and the further away the two burglaries were the less they seemed to matter, and the less likely to recur. A fire may happen twice in the same house, but it won't happen a third time; the principles of probability, though so wayward in their action, for misfortunes seldom come singly, were against it. Vivian increased as far as he could, his anti-burglar precautions; he lined his front-door and his two ground-floor windows with wreaths of protective and ornamental iron, as the Venetians, more practical in such measures than we, have always done, and he hoped for the best.

He realized, of course, that in a 'permissive' society, it was the victim, if so he could be called, who was in the wrong. He should have redoubled his efforts to safeguard his property against the very natural and, according to some psychiatrists, the almost laudable efforts of thieves to take it from him. When he came home, after dining with a friend, he surveyed with some satisfaction the intricate ironwork with which he had sought to thwart the thieves in their natural, praiseworthy impulse to get hold of him and his belongings. Permissiveness was the pass-word to today's society; and little regard as he agreed with it he felt slightly guilty for trying to stand in its way.

On the sideboard in his sitting-room still stood, among the other aperitifs, the bottle labelled 'Please do not touch'. No one had touched it except the rats and they were long ago extinct. When Vivian looked at it and saw the liquid was still half-way below the P of 'Please', he felt relieved and also (why?) a little disappointed.

Then came the night, for it was night about 3 a.m. by his watch, when the unexpected happened.

From his bedroom which was directly above his sitting-room, he heard noises difficult to describe; stealthy shufflings, furniture creaking, and occasionally a whispered word. What to do now? He crept out of bed, locked his bedroom door, fastened the window as quietly as he could, and returned to bed though not, of course, to sleep. The telephone was by his hand; should he ring the police? No; the intruders would hear and either make off with the swag or break through his bedroom door, enter (breaking and entering!), cosh him and tie him up. The police themselves said that in cases such as these, where dangerous criminals were about, discretion was the better part of valour. Pulling the bedclothes over his head he feigned sleep and only hoped that the tell-tale ticking of his heart would not be heard by those below.

Thus camouflaged from sight and insulated from outside sounds he himself could not hear at all distinctly. But, cautiously shifting the bedclothes, it seemed to him that the sounds underneath had ceased. No doubt the burglars had made off, taking with them what their predecessors had left them to take. Yes, the silence was complete. No use shutting the stable-door after the horse has gone; but Vivian felt that without danger to life and limb he could now dial 999. He explained what had happened; and the police officer said they would be round in a quarter of an hour.

These tidings gave Vivian a sudden burst of confidence, and not only confidence but curiosity. He would like to see what the thieves had actually taken; what they had left would be plain from the cloacal smell when the sitting-room door opened. Holding his nose against that, he gently pushed the door open.

But before he had time to shut it and flee upstairs he had taken in the whole scene, or some of it, the two masked figures bending over a third whose mask had fallen off, and who was lying on the floor with his arms spread out as if crucified, and his legs knotted together, crossed like a Crusader's so that they looked like one. The back of his head was towards the door, his chin tilted upwards. He looked like a butterfly on a stretching-board, and as motionless.

The two men who were bending over him jumped up. 'We'll leave him to you, governor,' said one of them, and before Vivian could answer they pushed him aside, made a dash for the front door which they had presumably forced open, despite its chevaux-de-frise defences, and the next thing he heard, for there was no sound in the room, was the whirr of their car starting up and fading away down the quiet street.

Vivian had little experience of death and didn't know whether the chin-tilted figure on the floor was dead or alive. Alive, he thought, for sometimes it twitched as a butterfly may twitch on the setting-board, long after it is dead. A sort of reflex action. But ought he not to find out? A revulsion seized him; why had this ill-meaning stranger chosen to come and die on him, if dying he was, and not already dead. Standing by the door, rooted to the spot where he had been pushed since he opened it and felt the rush of bodily-displaced air left by the accomplices, he felt an almost invincible reluctance to go further, to investigate further a region of experience as unknown to him as it was distasteful, and forced upon him by events. Yet it was not unknown; not many weeks ago he himself had lain on the self-same stretch of the self-same floor, struggling to free himself from his bonds, and growing feebler with every effort. It was an age of violence; but now it was not he but someone else who was demonstrating it.

Who?

A knock which Vivian didn't hear, and two policemen were in the room. The scene seemed so natural, so usual to them that their expressions hardly altered.

Fortified by their presence Vivian, who had been lingering in the doorway as a means of escape (upstairs? out into the street?), went into the middle of the room, and for the first time looked the burglar full in his upturned face. Distorted as it was, it was the face of a man he knew quite well; not a friend or an enemy, but an acquaintance whom he had sometimes met and exchanged a few words with at cocktail parties. The revelation came as a terrific shock, altering the whole current of his thoughts, and he clutched the table to steady himself.

The sergeant who was bending down with his ear to the burglar's heart, straightened himself.

'I'm afraid he's a goner,' he said, 'but we'll have to call an ambulance. May we use your telephone Mr. Vosper?'

'Of course,' said Vivian, surprised that the sergeant knew his name.

'They'll be here in a few minutes,' said the sergeant, putting down the receiver, 'but meanwhile may I ask you one or two questions?'

'Of course,' replied Vivian, automatically.

'I must tell you that anything you say may be used in evidence.'

'Of course.'

'This man was a burglar, there's his mask to prove it.'

'Yes,' said Vivian, looking down with a distaste that amounted to horror at the frail black object. 'There were two other men with him, also masked, but they made off when they saw me.'

'You were lucky,' the sergeant said. 'And now, Mr. Vosper, can you tell us anything more?'

Vivian suddenly felt faint.

There was whisky on the sideboard and another glass.

'Will you join me in a drink? But for God's sake don't take that one.'

He pointed to the half empty bottle, and the half empty glass, on the table.

'It's against regulations,' said the sergeant, 'but we won't say no,' and the three of them drank their whisky straight.

'Cheers!'

'I take it there's poison in that bottle,' said the sergeant, with his glass to his lips. 'Why?'

'Oh, for the rats. I've had a lot of trouble with rats, everyone in this street has. I've got rid of them all now.'

'All your rats?'

'Yes. Eight of them. Nearly all my neighbours have wanted to know my recipe, but they can't get the proper ingredients.'

'Why? Sherry is easy to come by.'

'Because chemists are more particular now than they used to be.'

For a few moments the three men sipped their drinks in silence. Then the sergeant said to his colleague with a grin,

'Tastes all right, Fred, doesn't it?'

Fred nodded assent.

'But if we both drop down dead,' said the sergeant playfully to Vivian, 'you'll be responsible, you know.'

'Oh no,' said Vivian, trying to fall in with his mood, 'because it isn't against regulations for *me* to drink.'

The sergeant smiled, and still with the smile on his face, looked down at the body crucified on the floor.

'You don't know who it is?' he asked suddenly.

Better not try to deceive the police. 'Yes, I do, he was a man I used to meet at parties, and who came here once or twice.'

'So he knew his way about?'

'I suppose so,' said Vivian. 'But there isn't much to know,' and with an inward-turning gesture he indicated the cramped proportions of his house.

'You didn't let him in, by any chance?' asked the sergeant, looking down speculatively at the body, one of whose outstretched hands, tight-fingered, might have been clutching the sergeant's chair-leg. 'He's a good-looking chap, or might have been once.'

'I don't know what you mean,' said Vivian. 'Between them they forced the door open while I was asleep in bed. That's all I know.'

'Forget it,' said the sergeant soothingly. 'No offence meant, but we have to ask these questions. You'd be surprised, Mr. Vosper, if you knew how many men living alone as you do, complain of burglars who aren't really burglars, but burglars by invitation, so to speak.'

'Then how do you account for the mask?' asked Vivian, looking at the fragile object which a draught from the two open doors was turning backwards and forwards.

'You never know what they'll be up to,' said the sergeant. 'A mask doesn't always mean what it seems to mean. I could be wearing this uniform'—he touched the medals on his tunic—'and not be a policeman at all.'

Vivian stared at him incredulously.

'Yes, it is so, Mr. Vosper, and that's why we can't leave any stone unturned. I'll take this'—and without any appearance of distaste, he stooped to pick up the frail object, which seemed all the frailer between his thick fingers. 'You can't tell me his name, by any chance?'

'I can,' said Vivian, and told him.

'I thought it might be,' said the sergeant, 'I thought it might be. We've had our eye on him for some time.'

'Shall I hear any more from you?' asked Vivian.

'You may—you may. But it won't be serious. You go to bed, Mr. Vosper,' said the sergeant, gently.

'What about the front door?'

'We'll fix it, and have a man on the watch.' He looked at Vivian again. 'You don't remember me,' he said, 'but I came here the other time you were burgled and beaten up and tied up. You were in a pretty bad shape, if I may say so.'

'I don't remember,' said Vivian, 'I don't remember much of what happened after they set about me.'

'I wasn't a sergeant then,' said the policeman, reminiscently, glancing down not without complacency at the three stripes on his sleeve. 'And I hope I shall be a Chief-Inspector before you have to call me in again, Mr. Vosper.'

The bell rang, unnecessarily, since the street door and the sitting-room door were open, and the sergeant's colleague let in two men who from their appearance might have been murderers.

'Just take him up,' said the sergeant, 'I don't think there's any need to be extra careful with him.'

The men bent down and their practised hands lifted the corpse, with as little expression on their faces as if they had been furniture-removers.

All the same, for Vivian, something went out of the room into the clear night air that wasn't a bit of furniture.

'There's nothing more, I think,' said the sergeant. 'You've got rid of the eight rats, or did you say nine?'

'Eight,' said Vivian.

'Well, I hope you won't have any more, Mr. Vosper. But just to make things straight, do you mind if I lock the door of your sitting-room to keep you safe and to let our forensic expert have a look at it? Just a matter of routine. He'll come early in the morning, before you are up, or down, perhaps.'

'By all means,' said Vivian, rising as the sergeant rose. They stood together in the passage, while the sergeant locked the sitting-room door and put the key in his pocket.

'Eight rats are better than nine, aren't they?' he said. 'Good-night, Mr. Vosper.'

'Vengeance is mine, I will repay,' saith the Lord. Vivian brooded on those words as he went upstairs to take his sleeping tablets. They didn't contain cyanide of potassium, but they were poison, all the same.

Revenge, revenge. It was an emotion as old as jealousy, from which it so often sprang. It was a classic emotion, coeval with the human race, and to profess oneself to be free of it was as dehumanizing, almost as much, and perhaps more, as if one professed oneself to be free of love—of which, as of jealousy, it was an offspring.

How many stories of the past, how many actions of the present, were founded in revenge. Vivian could hardly think of one that wasn't. Even the New Testament, that idealistic vision of the better world, wasn't free from it, or why should Christ have cursed the barren fig-tree? 'Revenge is sweet, and flavours all my dealings,' said, or sang, a character in one of Gilbert and Sullivan's operas, with playful irony, no doubt, but with a substratum of truth.

Vivian had got even with his tormentors, and the guilty had suffered for the guilty. *Ruat coelum, fiat justitia!* Justice had been done, and he, Vivian, had been its instrument.

Was it something to be pleased about, something to be proud of? He didn't know, just as he didn't know if the police-sergeant had accepted his story about the rats. He wasn't afraid of that. His daily help who, unexpectedly sadistic, had cut off and preserved the end of their tails, tail after tail on a string, because she said, and perhaps she was right, that rats didn't need telling twice, still less eight times, that a place wasn't healthy for them. She would confirm it; Mr. Stanforth, the porter, would confirm it; Vivian's rat-infested neighbours who had tried in vain to get his recipe for rat-bane, would confirm it. So the sergeant's suspicions, if he had them, could easily be allayed.

Would the human rats, the burglars who frequented the mews dwellings, be equally perceptive? Vivian asked himself. He couldn't hang up their tails because, as far as he knew, they hadn't any; but they had their bush-telegraph, just as the rats had, and the word would go round.

Vivian rubbed his shoulders and several other parts of his anatomy which still ached and perhaps would always ache from the attentions of the other gang of bandits, how many weeks ago! Well, if one bandit had paid the penalty and was now beyond feeling any ache or pain, so much the better for him. How and why had he fallen into this bad company? Why had he told them —mistakenly—since it had already been looted—that there was something in Vivian's house worth pinching? When he had come there once or twice for a drink, he must have noted an object or two that caught his connoisseur's eye. They weren't there now, nor was his connoisseur's eye, closed for ever in the mortuary.

In his medicine-cupboard, half concealed behind ranks of innocent medicines, was the half-empty bottle of cyanide which the police-sergeant had forgotten to impound.

On an impulse Vivian went downstairs. His sitting-room was locked against him but in the basement he found another bottle of Amontillado.

Corkscrew in hand he carried it up to his bathroom, opened the door and the window and set the tap running. Then with a trembling hand he poured out a measure of sherry into the wash-basin and replaced it with one of cyanide.

Who was this? Who was he? A Vivian he did not know. But as he stuck on to the sherry-bottle a label (in red ink this time) PLEASE DO NOT TOUCH, and cautiously sniffed the almond-breathing perfume, he had a sensation of ineffable, blissful sweetness.

HOME, SWEET HOME

IT was his old home all right, as he knew the moment he was inside the door, although who opened it to him he couldn't remember, for in those days of long ago who could remember who opened the door to him? It must have been one of his parent's servants who were often changing, and he himself wasn't a frequent visitor, he had been about the world so much; but the feeling, the sense of the house, as apart from its visible structure —the front hall, the inner hall—were as clear to him as they ever had been: as vivid as a scent, and not exactly a scent but a combination of thoughts, feelings, experiences, an exhalation of the past, which was as vivid to him now, and as much a part of him, as it had ever been.

He didn't ask himself why he was here—it seemed so natural that he should be—and then he remembered that he was expecting a guest—a guest for dinner, a guest for the week-end, a close friend of his, whom his parents didn't know, though they knew about her, and were expecting her, and looking forward to seeing her.

What time of year was it? What time of day? Dinner-time, certainly, for the light that filtered through the big north window was a diluted twilight when it reached the hall, revealing not so much the outlines as the vague, shadowy almost insubstantial shapes of the pieces of furniture he knew so well. And yet his inner mind recognized them as intimately as if they had been floodlit—perhaps more intimately, since they were of the same substance as his memory.

But while he was still under the spell of their rather ghostly impact on his consciousness, his awareness of himself as expressed in them, another thought, more practical and more immediate, penetrated it—where was Helen Furthermore, for she was the object of the exercise, and the reason why he had returned so unexpectedly to his old home? She needed looking after, and it was his job to look after her, for she did not know the rest of the party, who he somehow divined, were his relations, mostly older than himself, but he couldn't be sure, for he hadn't seen them—but they must be somewhere about—nor did they know her.

She might be late, of course, but she wasn't often late; she prided herself on not being late, but perhaps the taxi they had ordered for her—they must have ordered one—hadn't recognized her at the station, and she was wandering to and fro outside its precincts, with the desolate feeling that the non-met visitor has—what to do next, where to go next—for there wouldn't be another taxi at that wayside station. He could almost see her passing and repassing her little pile of luggage—not so little, for she never travelled light—growing more indistinct with each encounter in the growing gloom and more indistinct to herself, also, as the question of how to reach her destination grew more and more pressing until it began to occupy her whole being.

And then, quite suddenly, there she was—not in front of him, but behind him and round about him, a presence rather than a person. Someone must have let her in, as he had been let in, he couldn't quite remember how, because the front door opened on a little hall divided by a pair of glass doors from the middle hall where he was standing.

But it was she all right. He turned and recognized her not so much by her face, for it was covered by the dark veil she sometimes wore, but by the unmistakeable shape that was as much a part of her personality as she herself was.

'Valentine!'

'Helen!'

They must have exchanged those salutations and no doubt others, in a medium for him and perhaps her, of uncontrollable relief as if some terrible disaster had been providentially averted. He didn't see how, but he had the impression, that her impedimenta had been suitably removed; and the next thing was a compulsive necessity—for his mind could only harbour one idea at a time—to introduce her to her fellow-guests.

Why should they be in the dining-room and not the drawing-room? He didn't know; but he took it for granted that they were, and he was right, for when he opened the door for Lady Furthermore, he saw them all under the bright light of the chandelier, six or seven of them, seated round the dining-table, which was not laid for dinner, but rather like a board-room table surrounded by directors (bored indeed, for goodness knew how long they had been sitting there).

They all looked up and Valentine, who felt he must make an apology for himself as well as an excuse for her, said 'Here we are, late I'm afraid. This is Helen Furthermore,' and he was retreating behind her to let her make the effect which she always made, when the lights went out and the room was filled with darkness.

What to do now? Valentine's social conscience was still in the ascendant; come what might, he must introduce Helen to her fellow-guests. But how, when they were invisible even to him? No doubt the light would come on again. But it didn't, and meanwhile there was a slight muttering round the table which boded no good, as though Valentine himself had fused the lights.

It did not seem to surprise Helen to be ushered into an almost pitch-dark room, with in the middle a vague impression of heads and forms ranged round an oblong table. But she was noted for her social tact which had served her on many occasions more important, if less surprising than this; and Valentine, taking courage from her acceptance of it, with the additional encouragement of her hand in his, which nobody could see, began a tour of the table.

'Who are you?' he asked, bending over the first head that presented itself, if presented be the word, in the gloom.

'I'm your Uncle Eustace.'

'Uncle Eustace, this is Lady Furthermore,' (he hadn't meant to give her her title, but the situation seemed to demand it) 'who has come to spend the weekend with us, as I'm sure you know. May I introduce you to her?'

The head turned round, showing a pallid cheek, that certainly recalled Uncle Eustace.

'Of course, my dear boy, I am very happy to meet Lady Furthermore. I hope she will forgive me for not getting up, but in this darkness I feel I am safer sitting down.'

His voice quavered. How old could Uncle Eustace be?

'Please don't move,' said Lady Furthermore. 'I look forward so much to seeing you when . . . when the lights let me.'

Always groping, she and Valentine advanced a step or two. Then Valentine bent forward over a bowed head.

'Who are you? Please forgive me asking, but it's so dark I can't see my hand before my face—or your face,' he added, hoping it sounded like a joke.

'I'm your Aunt Agatha.'

It was rather annoying that 'they' should recognize him and not he them. But voices change; hers sounded very old.

'Dear Aunt Agatha. I am so glad to see you—at least I should be, if I *could* see you!' The joke, as he knew, fell rather flat. 'But I want to introduce you to a great friend of mine, Lady Furthermore, who has come to spend the weekend with us.'

'Lady Furthermore? I seem to know that name.'

'Yes, I'm sure you do.'

'She was a child when I—'

'I've always been a child,' interposed Helen, 'and I know that when we really see each other—'

'Yes? Yes?' said the old lady, who was obviously a little deaf.

'You will realize that you have weathered the storm better than I have.'

'Oh nonsense,' the old lady said. 'I can't see much, I couldn't, even if it wasn't dark—but I've never seen a picture of you since I don't know when that didn't look like what you have always looked like.'

'Thank you,' Helen said, more moved than she cared to show, but what matter since it couldn't be shown.

Together the two went on, addressing and being addressed, till they came to the chair at what must be the head of the table.

'Forgive me,' said Valentine, 'but who are you, if I may ask?'

'I'm your father.'

It took Valentine several moments to recover himself. He wondered if Helen had heard. 'Dear Daddy,' he began, 'this is a great friend of mine, Lady Furthermore. You've often heard me speak of her—'

At this moment there was an extraordinary noise between a crash and an explosion, and lights broke out, where it was impossible to say. Yet they were not lights in the sense that they banished the darkness: they were blue flares, wedge-shaped like arrows, piercing the room from end to end. And Valentine said to himself, 'Of course, it's the gas!' For many years ago, when the lighting of the house had been changed, much against his father's wish, from gas to electricity—'gas gives a much better light,' he used to say—he had a gas-bracket left in every room in case the electricity broke down, as he rather hoped it would. And now the gas—not like ordinary gas, but like flares at an old-time fair—was penetrating the room from every angle, blue arrows that like lightning flashes revealed nothing except themselves, and a sickly sheen of terror on the faces round the table.

Valentine grasped Helen's arm. 'Let's get out of here!' he said, and in a moment they were safe in the hall without apparently opening the dining-room door or shutting it.

Out of sight, out of mind. Valentine's memories of what had just taken place, perhaps from the excitement of the moment which often obliterates the details of a sensational happening, perhaps from some other cause, were already growing dim; they hadn't quite passed away, they had left a residue—of feeling? of sensation? of subconscious conviction?—that still lingered. The house didn't belong to him as he now realized, for there were other claimants. But he never suspected that it still belonged to his father. And this added very much to his new and growing preoccupation. Whoever might own the house, Helen was his guest as they all knew; and so far she had been treated very scurvily. She had not been shown her room: where was it? Upstairs, of course, but which room, the East Room? the South

Room? When he tried to think of the bedroom accommodation
and its access to bathrooms his mind became confused. All this
should have been arranged by whoever the house belonged to, his
father presumably, for his mother was long since dead—or was
she? She was not at the table with him, at least he didn't think
so, for he had not had time to complete his tour of introductions
round the table before the gas fireworks began. Somebody would
know, of course; but where was somebody? Where was any-
body? He had an invincible reluctance to re-enter the dining-
room with its shafts of blue light (*those* he *could* remember)
playing on the upturned, frightened faces of his elderly relations
and perhaps setting the house on fire despite his father's faith in
the innocuousness of gas.

The residue of these happenings in his sub-memory affected
his new preoccupation. Helen had not been treated in a guest-like
manner, and above all she had not been offered a drink. A long
cross-country journey and she had not been offered a drink! She
must need one terribly, just as he wanted one terribly; her throat
must be parched as his was, and with more reason for (so his
mental map told him) she had travelled much further than
he.

But what sort of drink would she like? That was one besetting
question. A gin and vermouth, a dry martini, his mind kept
repeating. But how could he ask her when he didn't know where
the drinks, if any, were kept? And a dry martini would be
specially welcome to someone whose system, like his own, was
already on the dry side? Vaguely, incoherently, came back to him
the memory of his visits to her, when drinks of all sorts were
immediately offered, and every provision for his comfort had been
arranged beforehand. And now this. He couldn't quite remember
what happened after her arrival; he didn't want to, it was too
mortifying, too humiliating. Could inhospitality have gone
further?

Where was she now? If she had vanished into the comparatively hospitable night, small blame to her; but no, she was
somewhere about, though he couldn't always locate her: some-

times at his back, sometimes on his left side, sometimes on his right, never in front, because in front of him was the large brass bowl? urn? container? which housed, as it always housed, the King Fern (*Osmunda Regalis*)—such a beautiful name, and it did not suit her. If only she would stop flitting and fluttering and let him have more than a side-glimpse of her! If only she would be more *stable*—for in ordinary life she was as stable as an anchor. At last she settled, like a butterfly; like a butterfly she was captive under his net.

'Helen,' he said, trying to see her expression under her veil, 'I feel so distressed about your visit, but I really couldn't have foreseen what was going to happen' ('and I can't now,' he might have added). 'But what particularly worries me is that you haven't had a *drink*. You must need one after your long journey, and I *want* one,' (this sentence had been repeating itself in his mind). 'But how, and where are they—the drinks I mean? The people are somewhere in the dining-room.'

He understood Helen to say she didn't care if she had a drink or not; but he didn't think this was true, and he himself was assailed by an appalling thirst.

Suddenly he had an idea which seemed like an inspiration flooding his whole being. The drawing-room, of course! Why hadn't he thought of the drawing-room? Before, it had appeared quite natural that Helen and he should have been received (welcomed was not the word) at a bare board in the dining-room; now it did seem strange when the drawing-room, the traditional place for hosts whoever they might be to greet their guests, was still available. And a vision of the drawing-room at once crossed his mind, with its cheerful yellow wallpaper counteracting its cold northern aspect, *and*, most important of all, in the right-hand corner facing the door, a gate-legged table bearing a tray of glasses and drinks, most of them non-alcoholic for his father belonged to a generation which had not heard of dry martinis, but had heard of whisky and sherry. Better whisky or sherry than nothing. The drawing-room was, for the moment, the only solution.

'Helen,' he repeated to the face under the veil, 'let's go into the drawing-room. We might find something there, something to drink I mean. And at any rate we shall be by ourselves.'

He thought her slight inclination of the head signified assent and so he led the way, up four steps and then to the right, to the drawing-room door with its pseudo linen-fold panels which were difficult to see because his father, economical in most ways, was especially economical about the use of artificial light.

Imagine their surprise, therefore, when the door opened to reveal a blaze of light—no fuse here—illuminating every part of the room from corner to corner and from cornice to cornice, and not least the cross-beams in the ceiling which an Italian crafts-man, early in the last century, had concealed beneath intricate designs in stucco. But before Valentine had time to do more than realize that the gate-legged table in the corner was still there, his eyes were astonished by another sight. So far, being of an accep-tant nature, he had taken everything that happened for granted, but now—!

There were six or seven little beds in the room, arranged side by side or end to end; and in each was a child, of indeterminate age and sex, asleep. Asleep when he and Helen came in; but when the light shone on their eyes they began to rub them, and having rubbed them, to set up a pitiful wail, each child taking it up from the next.

Beneath her veil which was so thick that even the brilliant light could not penetrate it, Helen's face was unreadable. I must get her out of this, he thought; this is worse than the dining-room. 'Please sit here,' he said, indicating a stiff-backed armchair which besides being the only chair in the room, commanded a view of the various beds, 'and I'll sit here,' and he sat down on the edge of the bed of a squalling child.

But before he and Helen had time to consult each other, or take in more than a tossing sea of bedclothes, a figure entered the room. It was a hospital nurse, dressed as such.

'What on earth are you doing here?' she asked.

Valentine, for the first time in many years, lost his temper.

'And what on earth are *you* doing here? What right have *you* to be here? This may not be my house, but it is the house of my family, the Walkovers, have you ever heard of them?'

The Sister touched her forehead, a gesture that might have meant anything.

'Yes, I have heard of them. Many years ago the Corporation—'

'The Corporation? *What* Corporation?'

'The Corporation. They bought this house from a family called Walkover, for a home for disturbed children.'

'Disturbed children?'

'Yes, here are some of them. And I can tell you that your unwarranted presence here is disturbing them more.'

Wails and screams gave credence to her words, but they only exasperated Valentine.

'I don't believe you for a moment,' he said. 'My relations are downstairs, and I'll fetch them up to tell you you are trespassing. Trespassing, do you hear?'

Having to make this scene in front of Helen aggravated his indignation. 'I'll order you to get out,' he shouted, 'and leave this place to whom it belongs. I came in here to get a drink for my friend Lady Furthermore—'

He wouldn't subject Helen to the indignity of introducing her to the Sister.

'There is some milk on the table in the corner,' the Sister said, 'and you are welcome to it, if you don't make too much noise.'

Valentine went to the table, seized a bottle of milk and hurled it at the Sister. A whitish streak, half fluid, half powder, such as might have been exuded by a bomber in the intense cold of the stratosphere—a sort of Milky Way—followed, until the missile struck the chandelier, and for the second time that night, darkness prevailed.

Helen was still with him; how they got out of the room he didn't know; how they got out of the house he didn't know; but he did know, or thought he knew, that he had put her on a train to somewhere.

'Where am I?' he thought, and then a sense of his proper environment—his bed—came back to him. 'But why am I so thirsty?' for he was longing, as never before, for a dry martini. 'Oh for a dry martini!'

The experience must have been real, from its mere physical aftermath; for never before had he waked up at night pining for a drink. He sat up in bed; where were the ingredients? They were downstairs behind a locked door; and the only thirst-quencher at hand was a long-opened bottle of sherry. He turned over and gradually his throat and tongue resumed their normal functions. 'I must have imagined it all,' he thought, 'and I hope that Helen has imagined it, too.'

With a vision of her stranded on some wayside railway platform, drinkless, even milk-less, it took him a long time to go to sleep.

'Anyhow,' he thought, 'she is well rid of Castlewick House.' He hadn't remembered the name of his old home until now.

THE SHADOW ON THE WALL

MILDRED FANSHAWE was a bachelor woman in her early forties. She was an interior decorator, and valued as such by quite a wide circle of customers and friends. But she was better known, to most of them, by her neuroses. Of these she pretended to poke fun, just as they, without pretending, poked fun of them to her. 'Have you seen a single magpie lately, Mildred? I mean a magpie without a mate?' 'Have you seen the new moon through glass?' 'Have you broken a looking-glass?'—'You must have, because looking-glasses are part of your stock-in-trade,' and so on.

If such enquiries were half teasing, they were also meant to be therapeutic, a way out for Mildred from the tyranny of her superstitions—if tyranny it was. Her friends were too fond of her to think she was making them up, much as they laughed at them. Laughter, even unkind laughter, they thought, is one way of curing an obstinate obsession.

But much as friends may laugh at you and much as you may laugh at yourself, it isn't an inevitable cure for something— difficult to define, more difficult to avow—which has got well below the surface.

Naturally in the course of business Mildred was asked to spend half-days or days or weekends with her clients or would-be clients. The day-by-day visits she didn't mind, indeed looked forward to them; but she rather dreaded the weekends, because when she was left to herself, especially in a strange house, her irrational fears were liable to get the better of her.

Her friends knew of this peculiarity and were tolerant and sympathetic, even while they smiled at it. 'We must have the house exorcised before we ask Mildred to stay!'

Joanna Bostock was a good customer and a good friend. Mildred had worked for her and knew her house well—that is to say, she knew parts of it well. The entrance hall was supported on each side by two honey-coloured columns that divided the main structure of the ground floor. To the right was the large dining-room with two long windows balancing the façade of the house; to the left was the main staircase, with its stained-glass windows, of Victorian date, and to the left of the staircase, a library and a drawing-room from whose doors, sometimes shut and sometimes open, Mrs. Bostock and her guests, when she had any, parted for the night, slowly going upstairs, politely making way for each other—'No, you, please'—until the hall was left unoccupied and Mrs. Bostock, or her butler, if she had one, turned out the light.

Mildred had been to Craventhorpe many times in the exercise of her profession, and knew its outside well. Around an oval patch of lawn crowned by a fountain said to be by Bernini, which was supposed to play but never did, a gravel sweep led to the front door. Long, low, and built of the most beautiful pink-red brick, this was the aspect of the house which was meant to catch the beholders' eye. Leaving her car, Mildred, who was by nature over-punctual, would sometimes walk to the left, where the west wing of the house, no less beautiful than the front, overlooked the garden and the tulip-tree, a truly monumental arboreal adornment which many people (for the house was sometimes open to the public) came from far to see. How it soared into the air! How its blossoms, not very like tulips, but near enough, gave it an exotic, an almost fabulous appeal! It was said to be the tallest tulip tree in England. Be that as it might, Mildred could never look at it without awe.

Generally, at this point, where the garden sloped down to a duck-pond, where the ducks were said to drown their redundant offspring, Mildred would turn back to the front door to announce her arrival.

But sometimes she made a circuit of the house. Its northern and its eastern aspects were very different—they were its *back* parts, they were almost slums! Joanna had never asked Mildred

what to do with these outside excrescences, botched up at such
or such a date and, architecturally, not fit to be seen. It was not
true, as some people said of seventeenth- and eighteenth-century
builders, that they couldn't go wrong. They built for show, for
outside or for inside effect. And if it didn't show, they couldn't
care less.

Craventhorpe was built in the shape of a hollow E; and the
hollow, over which the architects had taken no trouble, was an
eyesore to Joanna Bostock. What to do with it? Make it a sanc-
tuary for wild birds? But they had the pond to disport themselves
on or in and indulge their instincts. (She was fond of animals of all
sorts.) Or grass it over? Or make it a miniature maze with an
occasional garden statue, naked except for being bearded, leering
over the edge of the hedge at the visitors laughing, but half
frightened, by their efforts to find their way out?

Joanna hadn't consulted Mildred about this outside job, which
didn't need curtains or carpets or colours for the walls; nor had
she consulted her about the east wing, one side of which looked
down on the empty space, and was seldom used except for children and grandchildren. (Joanna was a widow whose husband,
dying young, had left her the house and the children to go with
it.)

*

Afraid of arriving too late, afraid of arriving too early, Mildred
was the first guest to be announced. (For some reason she was
relieved that Joanna had found a temporary butler.)

After the usual embracements, 'Darling,' Joanna said, 'I am *so*
glad you came before the others. Now come and have a drink, I
am sure you need one.'

She led the way to the library where the drinks stood on a glass
tray with gilt handles, a glittering array.

'Now what?' she asked. 'Which?' She had a way of making
invitation seem still more inviting.

'Oh, a very little for me,' said Mildred. 'Just some Dubonnet,
perhaps.'

Joanna poured it out for her, and whisky on the rocks for herself.

'Darling,' she said, 'I'm very glad you came early—you could never come *too* early—' She paused and added, 'You've never stayed here before, have you? I wonder why?'

'Perhaps because you never asked me,' said Mildred, sipping her drink.

Her hostess frowned. 'Oh no, I'm sure I've asked you scores of times. But you're always so much in demand.' She paused again, and poured out another tot of whisky. 'Isn't it awful how this grows on you? Not on you, dear Mildred, who dread nothing,' she laughed, a little tipsily. 'Not even a *mill*, and we haven't one round here, not to speak of, unless you dread a *thousand* things?' She laughed. 'Now what was I going to say?' She seemed to rack her memory. 'Oh, yes, our other weekend guests. I won't say who they are, even if I could remember, but you know most of them, and they will be overjoyed to see you, even if you—'

She stopped, and Mildred remembered Joanna's reputation for forgetfulness.

'So we *should* be eight for dinner, and I hope we shall be, but there's a man I can't rely on—he has some sort of job, half international, I suppose—you wouldn't know him, Mildred. He's called Count Olmütz—'

'No, I don't remember that name.'

'Well, he's an old friend of the family if I can call myself a family.'

'Oh, Joanna.'

'Yes, I mean it. But what was I going to say?'

'I've no idea.'

'Well, this man Olmütz should be coming in time for dinner'— Joanna glanced at the clock, which said 6.30—'if it's only to make the numbers even. We can have general conversation, of course, and you are so good at it, dear Mildred, but eight is a better number than seven, more cosy—and he has a lot to say, too much perhaps. But what was *I* going to say?'

'I've no idea.'

'Oh, now I remember,' Joanna said. 'I know you don't much like staying away from home.'

She stopped and gave Mildred a piercing look. 'But what I wanted to say was, you needn't feel nervous in *this* house. You have done *so* much for it, you know it so well. Indoors it's your creation, except for that eyesore that looks down on the court-yard—'

'I've seen it, of course,' said Mildred. 'I know the rest of the house much better.'

Voices could be heard in the hall.

'Well, what I wanted to say,' said Joanna hastily, 'before the immigrants break in, was, that in case you should be nervous in that long, rather lonely passage, I've put Count Olmütz in the room next yours, to keep you company, so to speak.'

'Oh,' said Mildred smiling, 'then I ought to lock my door?'

'Oh *no*,' said her hostess, apparently shocked. 'He's not at all that kind of man. I put him there well, as a sort of background, background music. He doesn't sing, but I'm afraid he might *snore*.'

'I remember the passage,' said Mildred, drawing her wrap round her, for the house, like many country houses, wasn't over-warm. 'You never asked me to do it up—perhaps you didn't want it done up?'

'Oh, I think it must look after itself,' said Joanna carelessly. 'A house is a hungry beast, and the more its appetite can be kept at bay the better. But there was something I wanted to say to you—can you remember what it was?'

'I've no idea.'

'Oh, now it comes back to me. This old friend of mine, Count Olmütz, is—what shall I say?—a man of irregular habits. Now, don't look alarmed, Mildred—not irregular in *that* sense, or I shouldn't dream of putting him within . . . within striking distance of you. No; I mean he's irregular in relation to the time-factor. I never quite know when he is coming, and I don't think he knows himself.' She heard a sound and looked round. 'Could that be a car driving up? Well, it might be him, coming back from one of his errands, his missions as he calls them. I hope he will be here for dinner because he's so amusing and will make our numbers even, but if he isn't, *tant pis*! He drives himself and may arrive at *any* time. We have that arrangement—*c'est entendu*—and the front door is always left open for him.'

'What, always, every night?' asked Mildred. 'Aren't you afraid of burglars?'

'Oh no, just at weekends, when he's able to get away. But he never knows when he can, and sometimes he arrives in the small hours. He's not in the least like a burglar. But if you happen to hear a noise in the night it will just be him, turning in, so to speak.'

Mildred thought this over.

'By turning in, you mean—'

'Oh, just dossing down for the night.'

'But won't he be rather disappointed,' asked Mildred, faintly malicious and slightly apprehensive, 'to find himself relegated, exiled to the eastern side? I mean,' she said boldly, for in these days one could say anything, 'wouldn't he rather be nearer *you* than act as the *preux chevalier* of an unknown female, in a remote quarter of the house?'

'No,' said her hostess, 'decidedly not. There are a good many reasons why not. I needn't go into them, but I can assure you that for everyone concerned, *for everyone concerned*,' she repeated firmly, 'it is the best arrangement. Listen,' she added suddenly, 'didn't you hear something?'

'You asked me that before,' said Mildred. 'There are so many sounds.'

At that moment the door opened and the butler said,

'Mr. and Mrs. Matewell, Madam,'

Joanna hastened towards them.

'Oh, darlings, I hope you didn't have too bad a journey?'

'Oh not bad at all,' said Mr. Matewell, a burly figure with a roundish squarish head to match, and dark hair growing sparser. 'Not bad at all except for a slight incident on the M4 which I'll tell you about.'

'Thank goodness it was no worse,' said Joanna, fatuously. 'Now here is Mildred, you all know each other.'

'Of course, of course. The maker of the home beautiful!' Mildred smiled at this pleasantry as best she could.

'And before we have drinks,' said Joanna, 'which I'm sure you must both be pining for'—and she led them towards the drink-tray—'shall I tell you who else is coming?'

'Please do!'

'The MacArthurs, that makes us six, Peter Pearson, such an invaluable man, seven, and . . . and—'

'Who is the eighth?' asked Mrs. Matewell, noting her hostess's hesitation.

'Oh, an old and great friend of mine, Count Olmütz. I don't think you know him.'

'No, but we've heard of him, haven't we, George?' said Mrs. Matewell, appealing to her husband, who seemed slightly at a loss. 'And we're longing to meet him, aren't we? He sounds such a romantic character. Didn't he own the house before you had it, Joanna?'

'No, he didn't own it,' said Joanna, shaking her head vigor-ously, 'he didn't own it, but he had something to do with it, I don't quite know what. I've sometimes asked him, but he's rather reticent. He may be here any minute and then perhaps he'll tell us. Ah, that may be him.'

It turned out, however, to be the MacArthurs, with the in-valuable Peter Pearson. 'Weren't we lucky?' Mrs. MacArthur said. 'Peter phoned us this afternoon and asked us if we were coming to you. I don't know how he guessed, but Peter knows everything.' Peter looked somewhat abashed but Mrs. MacArthur said 'We were only too glad to give Peter a lift.'

They settled down to their drinks and Peter turned out to be the life and soul of the party. 'I wish I could be two men,' he said, 'instead of half a man' (this shameless admission only evoked a giggle), 'because you're expecting another man, aren't you, Joanna, a real tough man.' He shuddered, albeit self-consciously.

'I don't think we'll wait for Franz,' said Joanna. 'He's so un-predictable.' She tried to keep the irritation out of her voice. 'Don't change unless you want to, but let's have our baths—if we want to. Dinner about eight.'

*

Dinner was a pleasant meal and no one worried unduly about the absent Franz—indeed, none of them except Joanna knew who he was. They had only heard tell of him, and if Joanna worried about him she didn't show it. Once, when his name came up, 'He's a law unto himself,' she said. About eleven o'clock they all retired for the night. 'You know your way?' said Joanna to Mildred.

'Oh yes, it's along the main passage, and then to the left.'

'I'll come with you,' said Joanna. 'Your name's on the door—I keep that old-fashioned custom—but you might not see it in this poor light. I hope your room won't be *too* uncomfortable—the bathroom is just opposite.'

They stopped where a sort of visiting card stuck to the door, 'Miss Mildred Fanshawe', made clear whose bedroom it was. 'And Franz is next to you,' she added, indicating his name-card, 'Count Olmütz'. 'Don't worry if you hear noises in the night. He sometimes comes in late. I'll leave the light on in the passage to guide him on his way—if it's turned out, you'll know he's arrived. Here is the switch if you want it, but I hope you won't. Good-night.' And Mildred found herself alone in her bedroom.

It was a comfortable room, with a wash-basin and mid-Victorian water-colours on the walls, but to Mildred's expert eye it sadly needed doing up—it was 'tatty'. Suddenly she had an almost irresistible impulse to look at the room of Count Olmütz, her next-door neighbour.

She would know if he had materialized because, if he had, the passage would be in darkness. But would it be? Might he not have forgotten to turn the light off? So unpredictable . . . Just one little peep behind the scenes . . .

But not now. It could wait. She must get ready for bed, a long ritual which included a bath. She always took a bath last thing, because it was said to be good for insomnia, and she had her face to do up. All this made bedtime a moment of crisis, a culmination of instead of a calm from the day's worries, which good sleepers have never known.

When she opened her door the darkness was almost blinding. She switched on the passage light and saw, outside her stable-mate's door, a pair of large muddy suede shoes. So the Count had arrived and she must restrain her curiosity. In English houses, thought Mildred, visitors don't leave their shoes outside the door, as they do in hotels—it's a sort of *nuance* that a foreigner might not know. The shoes were so muddy they needed cleaning, and no doubt the butler—the temporary butler—would see to that.

Why hadn't she noticed the shoes before? Mildred asked herself. And then she remembered that soon after she retired to her room, the lights in the passage had been turned off. Now they were on again—of course, she herself had turned them on.

What a fool I am, she thought, what a fool! But it wasn't the prospect of his over-large shoes which deterred her from knocking at his door, it was just his name on the plain card, fastened between four tiny triangles of brass, that made her hesitate.

She went back to her adjoining room, relieved as everyone is from the danger of self-exposure. She went through her customary bedtime ritual—with her a long process—but she knew she wouldn't sleep if she didn't. 'I'll have a bath first, she thought, 'and then a sleeping pill.' Insomnia was her bugbear.

The water was still hot—in some country houses it cooled down after midnight—and she lay with her eyes half-closed and she herself half asleep, in a bath of chemically-enriched foam. 'Oh to die like this!' she thought, though she didn't mean it. Some of her neuroses she had managed to overcome—the claustrophobia of travelling in a crowded train, for instance—and some she hadn't. A friend of hers had died in her bath of a heart attack. There was a bell over the bath (as used to be the custom) but when help came it was too late.

There was no bell over this bath, supposing there had been

anyone to answer it, but Mildred had long made a principle of leaving her bathroom door ajar. If someone came in—*tant pis*—she would shout, and the intruder, man or woman, would of course recoil.

It was well known that a hot bath was good for the nerves—so useful to have medical authority for something one *wanted* to do!

Mildred was luxuriating under the aromatic pine-green water, her limbs indistinct but still pale pink, when a shadow appeared on the shiny white wall facing her. It might have been someone she knew, but who can recognize a shadow?

It was Mildred's habit—unlike most people's—to have her bath with her head to the taps—and the shadow opposite on the gleaming wall, grew larger and darker.

'What do you want?' she asked, feeling a certain physical security under her opaque covering of foam.

'I want *you*,' the shadow answered.

But had he really spoken? Or was it a voice in a dream? There was no sound, no other sign, only the impress of the face on the wall, which every moment grew more vivid until its lips suddenly, like the gills of a fish, sprang open towards its snout.

Nobody knows how they will behave in a crisis. Mildred jumped out of the bath shouting 'Get the hell out of here!' And for the first time in many years she locked the bathroom door.

That would settle him!

But it hadn't, for when she came back from her physical and mental encounter with the key and looked round her with the ineffable relief of having done something that was hard to do, she saw the shadow, perhaps not so distinct as it had been, but with the upturning fish-like gills clearer than it was before.

So her way of escape was blocked: she was a prisoner now.

But what to do?

She got back into the cooling bath and turned on the tap—but no doubt in response to thermostatic control, the hot water was cooling too. Cold when she got out of it, she was colder than when she got in. Meanwhile, those thin, fishy lips gnawed at something she could not see.

Courage begets courage. 'I won't stand for this,' thought Mildred. 'I won't spend the night in this freezing bathroom' (actually it wasn't cold, but it felt cold to her). 'Take this, you beast!' and she flung her sponge at the shadow. For a moment its profile, which was all she had seen of it, was disturbed until the thin lips resumed their yawning movement.

What next? She hadn't brought her dressing-gown into the bathroom, it hadn't seemed necessary: she wrapped her bath-towel around her, unlocked the door, and plunged into the passage. The light was on; had it been on when she crossed the passage to the bathroom, half an hour, or an hour, ago? She thought not, but she couldn't remember; time was no longer a measure of experience to her, as it was after breakfast, with recognizable stopping-places—so long for letters, so long for her job, so long before lunch—if there was time for lunch. Nearly everyone divides their days into fixed periods of routine. Now these temporal landmarks had gone; she was alone in the passage, not knowing what hour it was.

But as a good guest she must turn the lights off. Had she left them on in the bathroom? She felt sure she hadn't, but she must make *quite* sure. With extreme reluctance she opened the bath-room door just far enough to peep in.

It was, as she knew it would be, in darkness; but she could still see on the wall facing the bath the last of the lingering image, lit up by its own faint radiance, its phosphorescence, but hardly resembling a face.

Had it been smouldering there all the time, or had it been re-lit when she opened the door?

What a relief to be back in the passage, under the protection of Count Olmütz, whose presence or whose proximity was to have saved her from these irrational fears! She had had them all her life, but never before had they taken shape, as it were, to her visual eye as they had to Belshazzar's.

When had he arrived? She had seen his shoes, his outsize shoes, when she first ventured on to the landing—prospecting bathwards. Then his door was shut, she could have sworn it; now it was ajar; but under the influence of any strong emotion, especially fear, time ceases to be a time-table.

She almost laughed when she remembered that she had asked Joanna whether she should lock her bedroom door! Some women locked theirs even when there was no threat of a nightly visitant, burglar, marauder, raper, or such-like.

She locked hers, too; but she couldn't lock out the sound from the next room—a sound hard to define—something between a snore, a gurgle, a croak and a gasp. She knew how throaty and bronchial men were, often coughing and clearing their throats and advertising their other physical ailments—a thing which women never did. She had always thought that a snoring husband would be better grounds for divorce than infidelity or desertion or cruelty—though was not snoring itself a form of cruelty?

How ironical that she should have to protect herself from her protector!

Happily she had brought her 'mufflers' with her (being a bad sleeper she dreaded casual or continual noises in the night). She stuffed them into her ears. But they didn't muffle the noise from next door; and suddenly Mildred thought, on her way from her dressing-table to her bed, 'Supposing he should be *ill*?' One thought of a protector as invulnerable to anything, especially to illness; but why should he be? He might have got 'flu or bronchitis or even pneumonia. Perhaps her hostess had put them side by side to protect each other, in that forsaken wing of the house!

However unconventional it was to beard a stranger in his bedroom, she felt she really *must* find out. Conscientiousness was part of her nature. Over-conscientiousness was the cause, together with guilt, of many of her neurotic fears.

Putting on her dressing-gown she went back into the passage. It was again in darkness, but she knew where the switch was.

What should she say to him? How should she explain herself? 'I am sorry to burst in like this, Count, but I heard a noise, and I wondered if you were quite well? Forgive me, I hope I haven't woken you up.' (This would be rather disingenuous, for the only deterrent to an inveterate snorer is to wake him up.) 'Oh, you *are* all right? There's nothing I can do for you? I am *so* glad, goodnight Count Olmütz, goodnight.'

She rehearsed these words, or something like them, under the bright unshadowed bulb in the passage; she made that movement of bodily tension known as 'pulling oneself together' that one often makes before doing something one dislikes. And then she stretched her hand out to push open the door which had been ajar; but it wasn't, it was locked, and no amount of rattling the handle (as if one wanted to break into a lavatory) would open it.

She could have sworn the door had been open, yawning, agape, the last time she crossed the passage; but how often had she crossed it? Fatigue and fear confused her memory; moreover, they confused as such things will her idea of what to do next, or what to do at all. But the stertorous sound, rising and falling as if a body was arguing with itself, came through the locked door plainer than ever.

Back in her bedroom she tried to reason it out. What should she do? Was it any business of hers if her next-door neighbour suffered from bronchial catarrh? Many people, many men at any rate, subside into wheezings when they lie down in bed. It was a sign of age—perhaps Count Olmütz wasn't very young? There was a bell in her room—there were two in fact—close by her bed, one of which said 'Up' and the other 'Down'. 'Up' would be the one to ring: presumably the household staff would be 'up' and not 'down'. But would they be 'up', in another sense of the word, at one o'clock in the morning, and would anyone answer if she did ring? And if some flustered housemaid—supposing there was one—appeared, what would Mildred say? 'The gentleman next door is snoring rather loudly. Can you do anything about it?'

It would be too silly.

'Leave it till the morning, leave it till the morning.' She had done her best, and if Count Olmütz chose to lock his door, it was no concern of hers. Perhaps he had decided to lock it against her, as she had once thought of locking it against him.

She got into bed, but insomnia is a relentless watchdog and

would not let her sleep. The sounds were growing fainter—the donkey's bray seemed to be petering out, when suddenly it took a new tone—a combination of gurgle, gasp, and choke, which made her jump out of bed.

It was then that she saw—and wondered how she could ever have forgotten—the door of partition, the door that divided her room from his.

She switched on her bedside lamp. She had her electric torch with her and she switched it on too. 'More light!' as Goethe said. The key turned in the lock, but was the door locked on the other side too? No, it wasn't; whatever his motives for secrecy, Count Olmütz had forgotten to lock the door on his side.

'I mustn't startle him,' she thought, putting her small hand over the torch's beam; so it was only gradually that she saw, piecemeal, what she afterwards thought she saw—the arm hanging limply down from the bed, the hand trailing the floor, the averted head and the familiar shadow on the wall behind— but with this difference that the gash, or gape, between nose and throat was wider than the fish's gape that she had seen before.

There was no sound. The silence was absolute, until she pierced it with a scream. For the head—the nearly severed head—was not the head of Count Olmütz, whoever he was; it was the head of a man she knew quite well, and whom Joanna knew quite well, in former days. There were all sorts of stories about him, some of which she knew; but she had not heard or thought of him, still less seen him, for a long, long time: not until tonight in fact.

But was it him? Could she be sure, she asked herself as with hands trembling with haste she began to pack her suitcase. A distorted face, with a gash under it, need it be somebody she knew? Recognition isn't an easy problem; on an identification parade could she have picked out a man, with his head thrown back and something blackish trickling down him, as somebody she knew?

No; but she dared not go back to confirm it or deny it.

She seized a sheet of writing-paper from the table at the foot of her bed.

'Darling, I have had to go. A sudden indisposition, 'flu I think, but I don't want to be ill on you, especially as I know you are going abroad next week. Lovely visit.' She hesitated a moment. 'Make my apologies to Count Olmütz.'

Like many women, she travelled light and packed quickly: then looked round to see if she had left anything behind. 'Why, I'm still in my pyjamas!' The discovery made her laugh hysterically. She slipped them off, put on her travelling attire, took a glance at herself in the mirror to see if she was properly arrayed for a long drive in the small hours.

Yes, she would pass; but *was* there anything she had left behind? The torch, the torch! She must have dropped it in her flight from 'the Count's' bedroom and she would need it to find her way through the dark passages, into the hall, out through the front door, on to the drive—left, right? right, left?—to the garage yard.

She couldn't go through these complicated manoeuvres without the torch, feeble as its ray was, and she must have dropped it out of reach behind the door of partition.

Sometimes clutching her suitcase, sometimes letting it drop on to the floor, she debated her next move, until dawn—like a picture frame—peeped behind the edges of the window curtains.

'Oh, damn it,' she said, and unlocked the dividing door.

There was a switch on his side as there was on hers, a device convenient no doubt for clandestine couples. Her fingers found it at once and light broke out, almost exploded from the central chandelier. What would it show? She only wanted to see one thing—her little torch. There it lay, almost at her feet.

She grabbed it, but in spite of herself she couldn't help looking round the room, dreading what she might see. But she saw nothing: nothing to alarm her, only an ordinary bed with the sheet turned back, so bravely, oh! not a crease, not a stain on it, still less a man under it.

'What a fool I am,' she thought, retreating to her room, but not forgetting to re-lock the intervening door or the door into the passage. The house was well supplied with keys. Just as, after a thunderstorm, one feels the weather will be settled for ever, she unpacked again, took out her pyjamas, made the necessary adjustments to her face, and slept peacefully.

The maid who brought her breakfast brought a note with it.

'Dearest Mildred, Do forgive me, but I can't say goodbye for I have to go away early—such a bore. Please ask for anything you want. Love, Joanna.'

*

Mildred called the maid back.

'You don't happen to know where Mrs. Bostock has gone?'

'No, Madam, she doesn't always tell us. I haven't seen her—she just left this note. Shall I draw the curtains, Madam?'

'Yes, please.'

How brave one is by daylight! Finishing her toast and marmalade, thinking how absurd even for someone who professed to be psychic, had been her visions of the night; she got out of bed, didn't bother to put on her dressing-gown, and unlocked the communicating door.

Night flooded in, hitting her in the face; but of course it would be dark for the curtains had not been drawn as hers had; no doubt the housemaid had been told not to call Count Olmütz, who arrived so late and slept so late. It was strange, after the cheerful radiance of her room, to be plunged into darkness again; strange and disquieting.

'Oh, why should I bother?' Mildred asked herself, with an eye on her dismantled suitcase, 'it's no business of mine.'

Curiosity killed the cat. It didn't kill Mildred, although what she saw seemed to have killed two people, if what they had given to each other was the blood that united them in a tangled coil, blood almost as dark and solid as to be snake-like.

Darkness gave way to daylight, and all was in readiness for Mildred's flight. Gratuity in hand, she muttered some words to the butler who had come to fetch her suitcase, words of thanks and words of warning, as casual as she could make them, and as hasty. 'The police, my lady?' asked the butler, wide-eyed. She some-

's job.'

come

I have

had no time to disclaim the title but said, 'Well, there is something *dripping* in the room next door; it may be a plumber's job.'

'Very good, my lady, but in my experience, the police come quicker than the plumbers.'

*

'Will the police find anything,' Mildred wondered, 'that I have found or haven't found?'